★ SADDLE ★

CHANCE OF A LIFETIME

From the battlegrounds of the Civil War to the California gold fields, the Saddle the Wind series sweeps you back through American history on an unforgettable journey. Each story has a very special heroine from a different time and culture, but all share a great love of horses and a unique brand of courage.

KINGFISHER
An imprint of Kingfisher Publications Plc
New Penderel House, 283-288 High Holborn
London WC1V 7HZ
www.kingfisherpub.com

First published by Kingfisher 2005
2 4 6 8 10 9 7 5 3 1

A CIP catalogue record for this book
is available from the British Library.

ISBN-13: 978 0 7534 1088 2
ISBN-10: 0 7534 1088 5

Printed in India
1TR/0705/THOM/MA/90GSM(W)/C

⋆ SADDLE THE WIND ⋆

CHANCE OF A LIFETIME

DEBORAH KENT

KINGFISHER

✳ Chapter One ✳

Slowly, reluctantly, Jacquetta May Logan walked from the barn back to the house. The July heat felt dense, like a thick cloud she had to push aside with every step. It had been deliciously cool in the woods, where the leaves and branches filtered out the rays of the sun. She'd ridden along a wide, shady trail on her bay gelding, Chance, breathing in the fresh air, grateful for half an hour away from the sewing room. If only she could have gone on riding till sundown, she thought. Aunt Clem would never allow it, of course. There was too much work to be done.

Sighing, Jacquetta slipped into the house

through the side door. She crossed the hall and headed for the drawing room, where the sewing table waited, heaped with blue homespun ready to be made into clothes for the family at Brookmoor.

Aunt Clem was there to greet her. "Jacquetta May!" she exclaimed. "Where have you been?"

"I went for a ride – just a quick one," she said. "I've finished the bodice."

Aunt Clem frowned. "I see you have," she said, holding up Jacquetta's work. "If you hadn't been in such a hurry, you'd have remembered the sleeves."

Jacquetta felt her face flush. "I'm sorry," she said. "I'll do them now."

From the far end of the table, Cousin Mattie offered a smile of sympathy. Jacquetta smiled back as she dropped into her seat. Dainty, golden-haired Mattie never slipped away from her work, Jacquetta thought, no matter how tedious the task or stifling the room. Mattie's thread never tangled or broke. Her hems were always beautifully straight, and her seams were almost invisible. Her needle darted in and out, in and out, leaving a chain of perfect little stitches in its wake. It hurt Jacquetta's head just to watch her.

Jacquetta found her needle where she had stuck it into a scrap of cloth. With a will of its own the thread twisted into a knot as she tried to slip the end through the needle's eye. Aunt Clem watched over her shoulder. "You're fourteen, aren't you?" she asked. "By fourteen, sewing should come as natural as breathing."

Jacquetta thought of the rake-thin, scowling sewing mistress at Miss Woodworth's Seminary for Young Ladies, the boarding school she had attended in Virginia. "At Miss Woodworth's they said I'd never be a seamstress," she admitted.

"What did they teach you then?" Aunt Clem wanted to know.

"French," Jacquetta said, with a little shudder. "Elocution – reciting poetry and making speeches. And deportment. Deportment every day." She'd spent endless hours walking with books balanced on her head to keep her posture straight, practising sitting and rising in her swirling skirts, and learning how and when to curtsey.

Aunt Clem shook her head. "All well and good," she said, "if these were ordinary times."

Jacquetta took up the panels of the bodice and

pinned on the missing sleeves. If she wanted to take Chance out for a longer ride today, she'd have to finish a presentable piece of work. She'd do whatever she had to do for a few hours of freedom!

Aunt Clem took up her own sewing again, to set the proper example. "We all have to work together," she declared, seated at the head of the table. "We're not just sewing for ourselves, remember. We're sewing for the Cause of the South!"

Jacquetta recognized the patient, resigned bow of Mattie's shoulders. After seventeen years on this earth, Mattie knew her mother pretty well. They were in for a lecture, and it might go on for hours.

"You girls should be proud of your heritage," Aunt Clem began, starting slowly, like a fiddler tuning up at a dance. "You come from the best stock in Mississippi. The Logans came out from Virginia when your grandfather was a little boy. They trace back to the best Virginia families, too. The Washingtons and the Madisons are some of your own kin, don't forget that."

Whenever Aunt Clem started to talk about fine

stock, Jacquetta couldn't help thinking of horses. The beautiful Morgans her father raised at Green Haven had a heritage to be proud of. Her papa had bought the stallion Samoset on a trip to New England, along with a string of Morgan mares. That had been back in 1849, the year Jacquetta was born. Now the Green Haven line was famous all over the South. You could tell well-bred horses by the way they held their heads high, by the grace and power of their movements. You couldn't miss their quick intelligence and eagerness to learn. Were there signs like that in people, Jacquetta wondered? If you lined up folks from three Mississippi families, could a stranger spot the Logans on account of their fine stock?

"That's why we're fighting this dreadful war," Aunt Clem went on, her voice rising. "The Yankees have no respect for our Southern heritage. They don't understand our way of life. And they think they can beat us." She struck the bell that stood beside her on the table and continued, "They think they can starve us out by blockading our ports. We can't import supplies, we can't sell our cotton, so they think they've got us in a corner. Well, they haven't got us. We'll make uniforms for our boys in the army. We'll make homespun clothes for ourselves. Every stitch we sew is an act of patriotism."

A black servant girl from the kitchen opened the door. "Yes'm?" she asked.

"Bring us some lemonade, and some of Ella's fresh tarts," Aunt Clem told her. As the girl disappeared she resumed, "We've all got to do our part. Even if it means doing chores we don't enjoy, we've got to pitch in for the Cause." Jacquetta struggled with her needle as Aunt Clem's words rattled around her. If you measured loyalty by how well a person did chores, she reflected, then she was a traitor to the Confederacy.

Aunt Clem's lecture finally ended when the servant girl came back with the tray. Sewing forgotten, Aunt Clem, Jacquetta and Mattie moved onto the veranda for their well-earned refreshment. The spreading magnolia trees created a semblance of shade. Jacquetta breathed in the scent of honeysuckle and gazed out across the rolling fields. Half a dozen of Uncle Silas's Jersey cows grazed quietly in the distance, down near the brook that edged the woods.

"Well, Jacquetta," Aunt Clem said, passing the plate of tarts, "you've been here a week now, haven't you? It's so sweet of your mama to loan you to us."

"Thank you, ma'am," Jacquetta said politely. "It's lovely to be here." "Loan" was an apt word to describe the situation, she mused. Mattie had been unbearably lonely here at Brookmoor, and Aunt Clem had asked Jacquetta to come for an extended visit. Jacquetta was good company for Mattie, even though Mattie was three years her senior.

The tarts were delicious, each baked in a crisp golden crust and still warm from the oven. Jacquetta loved the contrast between the sweet pastries and the tangy lemonade. She leaned back in her wicker chair and listened to the joyful song of a mockingbird. It was so peaceful here at Brookmoor. She could almost forget about the men off fighting and the Yankees with their cannons and cavalry. She could pretend they were still living back in the days before the war, when everyone was safe.

But she couldn't pretend the war away. If it

weren't for the war, her brothers Adam and Marcus would still be home at Green Haven. She never stopped worrying about them. Had any news come? Was Mama crying again, while she, Jacquetta, munched tarts on Aunt Clem's veranda? It wasn't right for her to be away at Brookmoor, where she couldn't know if some new trouble had hold of her family at this very minute. Somehow, the more she enjoyed her visit, the more she felt the need to go home again.

Away from the sewing table, Aunt Clem's natural warmth emerged. "Whatever happens, we've got to look for the silver lining," Aunt Clem remarked. "You're a silver lining for us in this war, Jacquetta May."

"Thank you," she said. "It's sweet of you to say so." After a moment she added, "Another silver lining is coming home from Virginia. The war let me get away from Miss Woodworth's."

It had felt like a miracle in February when Papa sent for her to come home, right in the middle of the term. It was the answer to her prayers. There was too much fighting in Virginia, Papa wrote. It wasn't safe for her to be so far away. Not that it was any safer in Mississippi, now that the Yankees had Vicksburg under siege. Sometimes they could hear the distant roar of cannonfire as they sat on the veranda at Green Haven. That was the real reason Papa had lent her to Aunt Clem now. He thought Green Haven was becoming too dangerous for his only daughter. Brookmoor was ten miles south, and further inland from the Mississippi River. The noise of cannons didn't reach them here.

Jacquetta had been overjoyed to leave Miss Woodworth's, to turn her back on French verbs and elocution, and most of all on deportment class. Sometimes Miss Woodworth's voice still chimed inside her head: "Say 'Yes, ma'am' and 'No, ma'am'." "Curtsey when you leave the room." "Sit up straight, Jacquetta! A lady always sits with her ankles together." Now, on Aunt Clem's veranda, she slid down in her chair and defiantly sprawled her legs before her so that her ankles showed plainly beneath the edge of her skirts.

Hooves clattered on the drive, and the wagon rolled into view with Uncle Silas perched on the seat. They hadn't expected him back from town until evening, bringing news and whatever supplies he could bargain for. He couldn't have gotten much business done in so short a time. Aunt Clem would start to scold and Uncle Silas would protest, and it all meant an end to these fragile moments of peace on the veranda.

Uncle Silas drew the wagon to a stop and climbed slowly down. Jacquetta saw that his hat was gone, and his hand trembled as he passed the reins to one of the stable boys. The boy began to unhitch the horses, a matching pair of black geldings called Jeff and Davis. Uncle Silas prized his team. He said President Jefferson Davis would be proud to know that such fine horses were named in his honour.

"Clementine!" Uncle Silas called. His voice cracked, and he tottered on his feet.

Aunt Clem sprang down from the veranda and rushed to meet him. "What's wrong, Silas?" she demanded. "What happened?"

"Grant's taken Vicksburg," he answered. "It's finished. They say in town—" He stopped, struggling for words. "They say blood ran in the streets. Like a river. A river of blood."

For a long, stunned moment no one spoke. Then

Aunt Clem began to cry. She and Uncle Silas stood with their arms around one another, swaying together in grief. Mattie reached for Jacquetta's hand. Mattie was crying too, but Jacquetta felt too dazed even for tears. Marcus and Adam were at Vicksburg. Were they all right? Had Mama and Papa heard any news of them? And if Vicksburg was in the hands of the Yankees, what would happen to Green Haven, only seven miles away?

That night Ella, the cook, served up a generous dinner of fried chicken and sweet potatoes, but no one took more than a few bites. Jacquetta looked desperately from her aunt to her uncle, longing for them to assure her that everything would be all right. Their faces were haggard with pain and dread. They gave no comfort, only a sense of foreboding she had never known before. She listened in horror as the dreadful possibilities unfolded before her.

"What's to stop them now?" Aunt Clem asked. "They'll burn our houses! Trample our crops and leave us all to starve!"

"Do you really think they'll come here, to

Brookmoor?" Mattie asked.

"From Vicksburg they'll have the run of the country," Uncle Silas said grimly. "I'll burn my cotton before I let the Yankees get their hands on it!"

Mattie began to cry again. "We'll all be murdered! I hear they kill Rebel babies! They stick them on pitchforks!"

Aunt Clem looked furtively around the dining room and lowered her voice. "What worries me — they might stir up the Negroes. Get our own servants to turn against us."

"Servants" was the word genteel people used when they spoke about slaves, Jacquetta thought. They were fighting this terrible war over slavery, yet most of the people she knew didn't even like to use the word.

All of the windows were open, but it felt as if there wasn't enough air in the room. Jacquetta longed to escape. She filled her mind with a picture that made her happy. She was back at Green Haven, and none of this was happening. The faces of her brothers floated before her. She heard Adam's teasing voice: "Go on, Jacquie! I dare you to jump the pasture fence!" She brought Chance to a steady canter, and then they were up and over in a glide so smooth she hardly felt the ground as they lighted on the other side.

Chance had been a present for Jacquetta's twelfth birthday. Back then he was a frolicking two-year-old colt who'd never felt a saddle on his back. Jacquetta used to bring treats for him out in the paddock – carrots and sugar lumps and slices of apple. She taught Chance to come when she whistled, like a big friendly dog. Papa and Adam helped Jacquetta train him to the saddle. The first time Marcus saw her ride the frisky bay gelding he clapped his hands and said she was born for the saddle.

The bright pictures faded away. Where was Adam now? He'd volunteered last October, as soon as he turned sixteen. Marcus, two years older, had already been in uniform for a year. Her mind formed a hideous question and she couldn't push it away. Had their blood flowed with that river in the streets of Vicksburg? She tried to imagine what they must have seen and heard – the roar of cannons, the choking clouds of smoke, the screams of men and horses dying in agony.

"I'm going back to the Mississippi Volunteers," Uncle Silas declared. "They've got to take me now."

"You can't!" Aunt Clem cried. "We need you here! Who's going to protect me and the girls?"

Uncle Silas seemed to expand in his chair at the head of the table. "The Mississippi Volunteers will defend our women and children," he promised. "Before the Yankees touch a blade of grass at Brookmoor, they'll have to contend with us."

At sixty-one, Uncle Silas was almost twenty years older than Aunt Clem, but that hadn't stopped him from trying to enlist when the war broke out two years ago, back in 1861. The recruiting officer had called him "Grandpa" and sent him home, angry and ashamed. It would be different this time, Jacquetta thought. They'd probably take any man who could hold a rifle. Her stomach gave a sickening lurch. They might even take Papa. His bad leg had kept him out of the war so far, but the army wouldn't be particular any more. Papa wasn't like Uncle Silas; he hadn't wanted to send the boys to fight, and he hadn't

18

wanted to go himself. He didn't talk much about patriotism and the Cause. Jacquetta almost believed he wished the South had never left the Union, though he wouldn't say such a thing aloud. She couldn't imagine him in uniform, limping along with his regiment, firing a gun at fellow human beings, even if they were Yankees. And suppose he was wounded! Or even worse...

The words tumbled out before she knew what she was going to say. "Aunt Clem – Uncle Silas – I've got to go home!"

For the first time they turned their attention to her. "Don't you even think of it!" Aunt Clem exclaimed. "The roads aren't safe. Besides, there's no one to take you. You'll stay here with us till this is over."

"I need to see my family!" she insisted. "I should be with them."

"Green Haven is even closer to Vicksburg than we are," Uncle Silas pointed out. "It doesn't make sense to take you back, it'd be like putting you right into Yankee hands."

"We're family to you," Aunt Clem said, folding Jacquetta in her arms.

Uncle Silas added, "Keep our Mattie company. Your papa will send word. Just be patient."

Jacquetta fell silent, but her mind went on working. She had to get back to Green Haven somehow. She would leave tonight, even if she had to go in secret. Out in the barn Chance was waiting. She and Chance would find their way home together.

✳ Chapter Two ✳

"Don't blow out the candle yet," Mattie whispered when they went up to their bedroom. "I don't want to be in the dark."

"All right. I'm wide awake, anyway." Jacquetta left the candle burning on the nightstand and sat on the edge of the truckle-bed. She pulled off her shoes but made no move to undress. Outside the window the night sounds were the same as ever – the whirring of crickets, the rustle of leaves in the breeze. An owl hooted sombrely from somewhere close by, and far away another called an answer. "I wish I was one of those hoot-owls," Jacquetta sighed. "Me and my family would live in a hollow tree. We'd never have to worry about the Yankees coming to find us."

"There could be Yankees out there right now," Mattie said, "putting a torch to the house."

"Cappy would bark and warn us," Jacquetta pointed out. They were safe at Brookmoor, for the moment at least.

Mattie lay back against the pillows in the big four-poster. She peered down at Jacquetta through the canopy curtains. "You always seem so brave," she marvelled. "Maybe it's from going away to that boarding school for a year and a half. Living up there with all those strangers."

"It wasn't so scary," Jacquetta said. "If you'd gone, you'd have done fine."

"Never!" Mattie exclaimed. "Nobody could make me go so far away."

Mattie had always been the timid one, afraid of venturing to unfamiliar places and meeting new people. She was the pretty one, too, golden-haired and blue-eyed as a fairytale princess. In contrast, Jacquetta had brown eyes and thick dark-brown hair. Long-legged and wiry, she always felt a bit awkward around her more delicate cousin.

If it hadn't been for the war, Jacquetta reflected, Mattie would surely have gotten over her shyness. She would have had invitations to all the balls and house parties in the Mississippi Delta. Sweet and pretty as she was, she'd have been courted by planters' sons from here to New Orleans. But there were no more dances, no more parties. The boys were off fighting, and Mattie Logan was left at home with no one to amuse her but her skinny younger cousin.

There was a long silence, and Jacquetta thought Mattie might have fallen asleep. She was glad for the stillness and the familiar night sounds outside. She needed time to think. It was true, what Uncle Silas said. The roads would be dangerous, and she'd be safer here than she would be at Green Haven. But if she stayed off the roads as much as she could, maybe no one would see her. She could be home by sun-up if she started soon. She'd have to be careful not to make a sound. If Aunt Clem or Uncle Silas woke up, they'd never let her go.

Mattie's voice crept through the dimness. "The Volunteers won't take Papa, will they?"

"If your mama has her way, he won't even get to the recruiting office."

"He's really stubborn," Mattie said. "He'll go first thing in the morning."

"They'll send him home, don't worry," Jacquetta said, but she wasn't so sure.

Her own father was only forty-six. He was quick and strong, even with his bad leg. He might feel it was his duty to sign up now, with the Yankees marching down from Vicksburg. Even if he didn't volunteer, maybe they would force him to enlist. Mama couldn't survive at Green Haven alone. At the very least, she'd need Jacquetta by her side.

The candle flame grew feeble. Mattie's steady breathing told Jacquetta she was safely asleep at last. In the fading candlelight Jacquetta wrote a hasty note: "I'm going back to Green Haven. I'll be all right. Thank you for everything. Love, Jacquetta May."

She wished she could tell Mattie her plans before she left. It didn't feel right to sneak off without a word. But Mattie would try to stop her. She'd be horrified by the idea of Jacquetta riding through the woods alone. No, Jacquetta thought sadly, she would have to slip away without even saying goodbye.

She wasn't afraid of travelling, not like Mattie was – but she had never travelled all by herself. The first time she went to Miss Woodworth's Marcus took her on the train, and Papa took her the next year. When she came home Miss Woodworth sent her with old Miss Clouder, the painting teacher. Papa had brought her down to Brookmoor. He had ridden Samoset, his beautiful sorrel stallion. Of course Jacquetta rode Chance. It was the longest ride they'd ever taken together, partly along the road, then cutting across fields and through the woods to reach Brookmoor by sundown. Could she remember the way? Could she retrace their journey in the dark, with Yankee marauders on the road?

The owl hooted again. Jacquetta didn't have time to wait. If she was going, she had to leave now.

Gingerly she picked up her shoes and got to her feet. For a moment she stood motionless, listening for any telltale rustle from the four-poster, but

Mattie's breathing remained steady and undisturbed. Carefully, with unbearable slowness, Jacquetta opened the door. She stepped out onto the landing and closed the door behind her with the same excruciating care. Sliding her hand along the wall she found the carved banister and started down the stairs. The third step gave a heart-stopping creak under her foot, and she froze, straining for some answering sound in the sleeping house. But no door crashed open, no one rushed onto the landing to demand where she was going. She kept to the edges of the stairs after that, and made her way silently to the bottom.

With memory to guide her she crossed the dark parlour and went through the sitting room to the dining room. She rounded the long table, careful not to bump against any protruding chairs, and located the door to the side yard. The key stood in the lock. It turned so stiffly that for one dreadful moment she feared the door would never budge. Then, with a grinding noise that set her teeth on edge, the door swung wide.

Jacquetta sat down on the porch and put her shoes on. A silver half-moon splashed the yard with welcoming light. A long shadow emerged from beneath the steps, and the air quivered with a deep rumbling growl. A dog stood staring at her, its eyes like tiny fires against the night.

"It's all right, Cappy," Jacquetta said softly. "It's only me. I'm no Yankee."

Cappy stopped growling. His ears pricked forward and his tail wagged gently. He gave a sharp, excited yip. In another instant he'd bark the house awake.

Jacquetta hurried across the yard to the outbuilding that served as the kitchen. Cappy followed close at her heels, watching every move she made. From a basket on the table Jacquetta grabbed a couple of biscuits left over from dinner. She looked around for more food that she could carry easily, and snatched up a handful of carrots. Tossing one of the biscuits to Cappy, she dropped the rest of the food into the deep pocket of her apron.

Cappy gulped the biscuit and looked at her expectantly, hoping for more. Jacquetta broke off part of the other one and held it out to him as she left the kitchen. The dog took the food and followed her across the yard to the stable.

The main door to the stable stood half open, and Jacquetta slipped gratefully inside. Cappy didn't follow her. The yard was his territory, and he stayed where he belonged. Jacquetta lifted the lantern that hung inside the door and struck a light. She breathed in the familiar scent of horses and hay. "Chance, it's me!" she called, her voice loud in the stillness.

From the third stall on the right Chance whinnied a greeting. He quivered with excitement as Jacquetta eased the bridle over his twitching ears. He must sense that something unusual is about to happen, Jacquetta thought. They'd never before gone out for a ride in the dead of night.

As Jacquetta led him out of the stall Chance nuzzled her hand, searching for treats. "You too?" Jacquetta said, laughing. "You're as bad as the dog!" She took a carrot from her apron and felt the horse's velvet nose brush her fingers. With a satisfied crunch the carrot disappeared.

Jacquetta crossed to the rack of saddles on the wall. Automatically she reached for the side-saddle she had used on the ride from Green Haven. A properly raised girl was always supposed to ride side-saddle, her skirts folded neatly around her legs, as though she were still in the sitting room. Side-saddle was fine for a sedate outing along a country lane. It was less comfortable when the terrain got rough, and it would be easier to stand in the stirrups – or if the horse broke unexpectedly into a gallop. Boys had all the advantages, riding astride.

Jacquetta's hands fell to her sides. She eyed the men's saddles longingly. She knew how to ride astride. Adam had dared her to try, and she could never refuse a dare from Adam. It had felt strange for a few moments, her legs wide apart, knees gripping Chance's flanks. Then, as Chance trotted out of the corral, Jacquetta's spirit had soared. She pressed lightly with her heels and urged him into a canter. This was more like flying than riding. Surely this was what riding was meant to be!

She couldn't afford to ride through the woods like a lady tonight. Maybe she would have to urge Chance to top speed, with a band of Yankees in pursuit. She would need strength and agility and every bit of skill she could muster.

Jacquetta left the side-saddle hanging on its peg and chose the oldest, most worn men's saddle in Uncle Silas's barn. The war gave her permission, she told herself. The side-saddle was meant for ordinary times.

They were nearly ready now. Jacquetta scooped a few handfuls of oats into a leather pouch and stuffed it into one of the saddlebags. She blew out the lantern and hung it back on its peg. As Cappy watched intently, she led Chance through the paddock and clicked the gate shut behind them. Then, hopping onto the mounting block, she sprang into the saddle. Gathering her long skirt out of the way as best she could, she slid her feet into the stirrups.

Chance stood poised, waiting for orders. Jacquetta clicked her tongue and gave a light touch with her heels. Chance set off at a smooth, easy walk.

Behind them Cappy broke into a din of barking. It wouldn't be long before Uncle Silas hurried down to investigate. Aunt Clem and Mattie would wake up too, and Mattie would see that the truckle-bed was empty. She'd find

Jacquetta's note, and take it straight to her mother and father. Uncle Silas would wake the servants and organize a search party. They'd keep looking till they found her and brought her safely back to Brookmoor.

"Come on, Chance! Faster!" she cried. She gave the horse a sharp kick and they surged ahead.

When they reached the brook at the bottom of the field, Chance hesitated. He was always a little uneasy about bridges. Maybe it scared him to look through the cracks between the planks and see water below. He touched the bridge with a tentative hoof and turned his head to look at Jacquetta. "It's fine, boy. Go ahead," she said in her most reassuring voice. To her relief, he took her at her word. His hooves clattered over the bridge.

As the woods closed around them they were forced to slow down. Leafy branches brushed Jacquetta's face. She bent low along Chance's neck to avoid being cracked on the head by an overhanging limb. She could hardly see the path in the moonlight, but somehow Chance's hooves found the way. Cappy's barking faded. Soon there were no sounds but the rasp of crickets and the lonesome calls of the owls.

Jacquetta guessed she'd been riding for about an hour when the path disappeared altogether. She drew Chance to a stop and sat still, fighting her rising panic. The woods stretched around them in every direction, vast and mysterious. She'd once heard of a woman who got lost berry-picking and wandered in circles for days until someone found her, half-starved and crazy with terror, cowering in a thicket. Maybe that was the fate that awaited Jacquetta May Logan. Maybe that's what she deserved for running off from Aunt Clem and Uncle Silas on her own. No proper young lady would have dreamed of such a thing!

If she turned back, she could find the path again. Maybe she'd meet whatever search team Uncle Silas had sent out from Brookmoor. It would be better than starving or being attacked by a wildcat. But she didn't want to go back to Brookmoor. She wanted to go home.

She sat motionless, the reins loose on her lap, and tried to think clearly. She knew they'd been heading north when they crossed the brook. The path had curved here and there, but it had taken them more or less in the same direction. When she and her father crossed the fields they'd been riding east, the afternoon sun at their backs. Then they'd turned south along the path through the woods. The field must border the woods to the west. Once she found it, she'd be able to find the road.

Jacquetta picked up the reins again and tried to turn Chance to the left. Usually he responded eagerly to her commands, but this time he resisted. After a few moments Jacquetta eased up on the reins and let the gelding have his way. Placing his feet carefully among the tangles, Chance set off through the trackless woods. He was still moving northward, as far as Jacquetta could tell. It seemed like a difficult route, but maybe it was the most direct one. Besides, the more they kept to the woods, the less likely they were to run into a Yankee scouting party.

Jacquetta let the reins fall slack and trusted Chance to make the decisions. Briars clawed at her skirt, and clouds of mosquitoes whined around her ears. Once, Chance came to a halt, his head high and nostrils flaring as though searching for some signal on the night air. Then he made a sharp turn to the right and set off again, his gait full of purpose.

Wherever Chance was taking her, they weren't getting there in a hurry. The gelding fought his way through the brush, zig-zagging around the densest clumps of bushes and stepping daintily over fallen logs. Jacquetta grew tired of fending off branches. She slid to the ground and walked behind Chance in single file. They ought to have reached the field by now. The woods seemed to have grown wider and thicker overnight, engulfing every landmark. She and Papa had followed a clean, well-worn path when they went to Brookmoor. Where had it disappeared? The woods could hide anything – bears and wildcats, rattlers and Yankee soldiers. Was it true what Mattie said, that the Yankees liked to spear Rebel babies on pitchforks? What would they do to an unprotected Rebel girl of fourteen?

The first streaks of dawn brightened the sky, and Jacquetta realized that now they were heading west. As the morning birds stirred and twittered, she felt a glow of relief. Somehow Chance knew where he was going. Jacquetta understood that he wanted to get home as badly as she did herself. He wanted to be back in his familiar barn, to go back to the field where he'd played as a colt, where he still loved to run free. Chance would find the way.

The trees began to thin. Jacquetta let Chance nose some oats out of the pouch, a well-earned reward for his night's work. Patting the gelding's neck fondly, she climbed into the saddle again. In a few minutes they emerged from the woods into a broad meadow. Drawing Chance to a stop, Jacquetta gazed around her. A rail fence skirted the meadow in front of them, and beyond it in the far distance she was sure she saw a line of moving specks, one behind the other. They could only be wagons travelling along a road. Jacquetta knew this half-fenced meadow and that stretch of road. She knew exactly where they were at last – they'd reached the Clarence place, the neighbouring plantation just south of Green Haven.

"Chance!" she exclaimed. "We're almost home!"

Chance's ears cocked forward, and he gave a little prance of excitement. But something wasn't right. Those wagons looked too big, the line was too orderly, and it went on and on. Papa didn't own a string of wagons like that. Neither did any of the planters in this part of the country. That steady procession might be carrying supplies to the Rebel forces, the battered survivors of Vicksburg. Or those could be Yankee wagons, supplying food and shells to the Union troops.

Her heart racing, Jacquetta rode across the Clarences' meadow. The ground dipped and rose again. From the top of the next knoll she'd be able to see Green Haven. She'd see the main house, the cotton fields, and the tree-lined drive looping in from the road. Maybe she'd see Papa himself. He was always an early riser. He'd be out talking to the overseer, giving instructions for the day's work. What would he say when she rode up to him? He wouldn't scold her, she was certain. He'd be amazed at first, and overjoyed that she was home safe.

Chance broke into a fast trot that carried them to the top of the knoll. Jacquetta reined him in and gazed out over the plantation where she had been born. Through a strange, gauzy haze she saw the distant outline of the big house. An acrid smell of smoke hung in the air. The cotton fields, that should have been a rolling sea of white, lay in blackened ruins.

Uncle Silas's words rushed back to her: "I'll burn my cotton before I let the Yankees get their hands on it!" Someone had set fire to the cotton at Green Haven.

Papa would never burn his crop, not even to keep it from the Yankees. Where was Papa now? Where was Mama? Something terrible had happened here while she was safe at Brookmoor.

⋆ Chapter Three ⋆

For an instant Chance stood stock-still. His nostrils flared as he caught the smell of burning. Jacquetta felt a shiver run through him, as though all his muscles drew tight as a bowstring. Then, before she could take in a breath, he whirled and headed back across the field at a break-neck gallop.

"Whoa!" she cried, hauling on the reins. Chance didn't seem to hear her. Jacquetta stood in the stirrups and pulled with all her strength, but the horse plunged forward as though he didn't even feel the bit.

Chance's flight caught Jacquetta completely off guard. Her bones rattled with every jolt and leap.

When he swerved sharply to the right she nearly slid down his left shoulder. Her right foot lost its stirrup. Gripping with her knees, clutching handfuls of mane, she searched for the stirrup in vain. "Whoa, Chance!" she kept screaming. "Steady, boy! Steady!" She'd have to calm herself down before she could hope to bring Chance under control. But the long desperate night and the shock of those clouds of smoke had undone her. She couldn't think. She could only shriek with each breath she drew, "No! Stop! Chance, stop!"

Afterwards, she couldn't remember falling. Suddenly the earth slammed her with a full body blow. Somehow she had kicked her left foot free of the remaining stirrup and lay still as Chance's hoofbeats pounded into the distance. It felt good not to move. She didn't have to hang on any more. She didn't have to wonder what she ought to do next. She could simply lie still, wherever she was. This moment, right now, was all that mattered.

The world came back slowly, a little piece at a time. She became aware that she was lying in thick, prickly grass. For a while she couldn't figure out where all the pain was coming from. She had landed on her left side, and it felt bruised and skinned from shoulder to toes. After a careful inventory of her body parts she realized that the worst of the pain was centred in her hip. She felt it with cautious fingers, half dreading to discover ragged bone protruding through her skin. She found a very large sore spot, but her bones seemed to be where they belonged.

Shakily she pushed herself up until she sat with her legs outstretched, leaning back on her undamaged right hand. Thoughts crowded into her head, clamouring for attention. Papa's cotton was gone – burned – all the season's hopes charred and smoking in the field behind her. It was true, then: the Yankees had come to Green Haven. Perhaps they had moved on to work their mischief somewhere else. But maybe they were still here. At any moment a Yankee soldier might march across the Clarences' pasture and spot her sitting here, bruised and battered, in her tangle of skirts. She was too tired to run. Her hip throbbed too badly. But if she gave herself up, what would they do to her?

If only Papa would come! Calm and solid, Papa would comfort her and bring order back to the world. He must be busy taking care of Mama, wherever they were. Poor Mama was always imagining disasters, and now a real calamity had landed on their own doorstep. Had Mama cried when the Yankees came? Had she fallen down in a faint? Did the Yankees take pity on her, a frightened defenceless woman? Or were they as cruel as Mattie and Aunt Clem said they were?

The more she thought of Papa and Mama, the more desperately alone she felt. She had no one to turn to, no one to tell her what she needed to do. Even Chance had deserted her, galloping away with an empty saddle.

Something tickled her hand. Jacquetta glanced down and saw a tiny white spider walking daintily across her knuckles. As she watched, a puff of breeze lifted it up and away. It settled on a grass stalk a few inches off and went on with its delicate dance as though nothing had happened.

She was a lot like that spider, Jacquetta thought miserably. The war had picked her up and dropped her here as if it were some giant wind. But she couldn't resume where she'd left off. Not one thing remained the same. She couldn't be sure of anything.

But she wasn't a little white spider, Jacquetta told herself sternly. The war was a force she could not control, but she could still make decisions. She had decided to leave Brookmoor and return to Green Haven. Now she had to figure out what to do next.

She would start with Chance.

Chance hadn't set out to hurt her, she knew. Any horse would bolt at the smell of smoke. Chance had expected fresh oats and clean straw at the end of their nighttime journey. Instead he found fire, the danger horses fear above any other. No wonder he forgot all his training. No wonder he fled!

Pushing hard with her right leg, easing up on the left, Jacquetta got to her feet. She tilted back her head and let loose the whistle she had taught Chance to recognize. Its two notes, rising like a question, floated out toward the woods. She waited a few moments, then whistled again. Again she waited. From somewhere far away came the thud of a horse's feet. Chance's head appeared above the bushes.

The horse approached cautiously. His nostrils flared, his ears flicked back and forth, and he walked as though he didn't quite trust the ground. He had fled from the smell of smoke, and now he was returning, drawing closer to the danger with every step. She had called, and he was coming back. Jacquetta held out her hand and waited.

At last the gelding's velvet nose touched her fingertips. "Good boy, Chance," she murmured. "We'll be all right. Don't you worry now!"

For a few moments she leaned against Chance's shoulder. He stood motionless, warm and solid and reassuring. In his own way, he was telling her that it was true – yes, they would be all right. Somehow.

Her apron pocket was empty. The last of the carrots had scattered when she fell. Jacquetta searched in the grass until she found one, broken and spattered with mud. Chance was happy to have it. In two crunches it was gone, and he nuzzled her hand for more.

"That's all," she told him. "Sorry." Her own

stomach gave a lurch of hunger. She pictured steaming hotcakes drenched with honey, mounds of scrambled eggs and strips of salty ham. Then she thought of her bed with its flowered counterpane and the ruffled pillows Mama had ordered all the way from France. She didn't know which she longed for most – food or sleep. Well, she told herself sternly, she was in no position to get either one right now. She had to learn whether her parents were safe.

Jacquetta unsaddled Chance and rubbed him down as well as she could with handfuls of grass. Then she led him to a shallow stream at the edge of the field. When he had drunk his fill she found a small clearing in the woods and knotted his reins over a tree limb. "I'll be back in a little while," she told him, and left him cropping the grass contentedly.

The sky was clear and bright now, and Jacquetta couldn't approach the house without being seen. Her best plan, she decided, was to keep watch for a while and observe who came and went. Keeping to the shelter of the woods she skirted the fields. The smoke stung her eyes as she passed the blackened cotton. She didn't want to look, but she couldn't turn away. Not everything had burned, she saw now. The edges closest to the woods were reduced to charred stubble, but further off the cotton was still standing, untouched. It looked almost as if someone had rushed to put out the flames.

Red and massive, the barn looked just as it had when Jacquetta had left a week ago. She couldn't see the big house yet, and she didn't dare go much nearer.

Close beside the barn grew a sturdy apple tree. It was the best climbing tree at Green Haven. Jacquetta had spent countless hours in its branches, reading a book or spying on Marcus when he and his sweetheart Janie Amberson were together down in the yard. Once she'd thrown an apple at Marcus's head just as he and Janie were about to kiss. For a moment Jacquetta remembered the astounded look on her brother's face — quiet, serious Marcus, who'd probably spent all week working up the courage to kiss his girl.

This was no time for looking back. Gathering up her skirts Jacquetta broke from the woods with a burst of speed. In seconds she crossed an open patch of yard and swung herself onto the bottom limb. Ignoring her throbbing hip she scrambled up to a fork that was level with the barn roof. She had a perfect view of the back of the house, and the thick leaves hid her from a casual glance. No one would spot her unless they were trying to find her – and so far nobody knew she was here to find.

For the first few seconds she saw an ordinary Green Haven morning. The house was quiet, barely awake. A few chickens pecked in the yard outside the kitchen, and Adam's old hound, Silver, rolled in the dust. Iza, the cook, and a young girl, one of her helpers, stepped out of the kitchen and stood talking in the kitchen garden. Jacquetta couldn't catch their words, only the murmur of their voices on the wind.

The soldier was standing so still that at first she didn't see him at all. He leaned against a corner of the house, half hidden by a big lilac bush. A rifle rested on his right shoulder. He wore the blue uniform of a Yankee.

Jacquetta's heart pounded wildly. She gripped the branch beside her until the rough bark bit into her hands. He must be a sentry, standing on guard duty. He'd sound an alarm – or shoot – if he saw anyone approach. He was there to defend Green Haven – from its neighbours, from Confederate troops, from the family that rightfully belonged there.

For a mad moment Jacquetta wanted to hurtle down from her tree, rush to the Yankee sentry and demand to know what they had done to Mama and Papa. If her parents were prisoners, she could be a captive alongside them. At least they would be together, whatever happened.

No, she told herself fiercely, she would never put herself into the hands of those thieves and murderers. If Mama and Papa were locked up somewhere, she'd find a way to rescue them. Her mind made one frantic leap after another. She'd go to the Clarences for help. Or sneak into the house at night, find her parents, and cut the ropes that bound them. Or she'd ride back to Brookmoor and get Uncle Silas with his Mississippi Volunteers.

The back door opened, and two more Yankee soldiers stepped into the sunlight. Silver broke into a shrill bark, but he cowered at the same time. He acted frightened, as though he expected to be kicked.

The soldiers sauntered across the yard to the barn door. "No," said one, in a clipped Yankee accent. "You can't take them today. We're going to have our hands full pretty soon." He was a thick, stubby man who puffed on a pipe.

"Then tomorrow will be even worse," said the second man.

"We'll know how many more wounded we've got and we'll know how bad they are," said the one with the pipe. "Maybe we can spare you then."

"It doesn't have to be me. Send somebody else. Morton needs every horse he can get his hands on." The second man was thin, with a lined, troubled face. What struck Jacquetta most was his flaming red hair. She had never before seen anyone with hair quite that colour.

"He took twenty-three yesterday. He's not hurting," said the man with the pipe.

The red-haired man looked unhappy. "He needs the rest," he muttered. "Today."

The man with the pipe gave a sigh. "I hate to

send them," he said. "They won't last a month out there. And they're such beauties! Morgans all the way!"

The red-haired soldier shrugged. "They can carry supplies. Haul wagons. That's what counts." Their voices faded as they disappeared into the barn.

With a sickening twist in her stomach, Jacquetta realized what the soldiers intended to do. They were going to steal the horses and give them to the Yankee army! She'd heard of that kind of horse-stealing before. The Confederate army did it, too. Soldiers didn't call it stealing; they said they were "commandeering" the horses, because the army needed them so badly.

Jacquetta had heard what happened to cavalry horses ridden by soldiers, and to the horses that pulled heavy wagons loaded with food and tents and ammunition. The army worked them to exhaustion. Though they neighed in terror they were forced into battle. And in the fighting they were slaughtered. As the war ground on, so many horses died that the armies constantly needed more. If the Yankees came upon horses in a town or on a farm, they'd commandeer them on the spot. Jacquetta thought of the horses at Vicksburg, screaming and bleeding and dying in agony, along with the soldiers. They'd been torn from their fields and stables and sentenced to die, through no fault of their own.

Now the Yankees meant to commandeer Papa's horses. They'd taken twenty-three already. Which of them were still here, waiting to be led away to their doom?

An even more dreadful thought seized her. If they found Chance, the Yankees would commandeer him, too.

It seemed a long time before the two Yankees emerged from the barn. They nodded to the sentry and went back into the house. Iza and the servant girl had returned to the kitchen. Only the clucking of hens and the occasional crow of a rooster broke the stillness.

Jacquetta slid to the branch below and inched along it toward the barn wall. The branch brought her just within reach of a narrow window. As she had done dozens of times before, she grabbed the sill and squeezed through the opening. Softly she dropped onto the prickly bales of hay in the loft. The hay rustled as she crawled to the trapdoor and looked down. She couldn't see much in the dimness. Only one stall was visible, no matter how she craned her neck. It was Samoset's stall, the first one in from the door. Above the half-door the stallion's golden head stretched up as if to greet her. Samoset was still safe!

She was safe herself, for the moment at least. The hayloft was snug and quiet. She could curl up and sleep. Maybe when she woke her mind would be clearer, and she'd know what to do next.

Jacquetta was about to crawl back into a corner of the loft when a shadow fell across the open barn door. The slender figure of a girl entered and paused at Samoset's stall. "Hey you, big fella," crooned a soft voice. "I brung you some sugar."

It was Iza's helper, the girl she'd seen in the kitchen garden. Jacquetta knew she'd seen her at Green Haven before, but she couldn't remember her name. The girl left Samoset and vanished from Jacquetta's line of vision, but Jacquetta could still hear her talking. "There you go, Tina! Sugar for you, too... Don't you worry none, Dorcas! Yours is right here!... Hold still there, you! You 'bout made me drop it in the straw!"

Dorcas was still here, and Tina – and how many others? This girl could answer all her questions. She'd been here when the Yankees came. She must know what had become of Mama and Papa.

In her eagerness, Jacquetta didn't think any further. She was halfway down the ladder before she realized that one of the soldiers might walk in at any moment. She froze, gazing out through the wide-open door. Her foot scraped on the ladder and the girl looked up with a gasp. "Miss Jacquie?" she exclaimed in amazement. "My Lord, you 'bout scared me to death!"

"Ssh!" Jacquetta whispered, gesturing frantically. "You've got to help me! Don't let anyone know I'm here!"

⋆ Chapter Four ⋆

"What you doin' here?" the girl asked, staring at Jacquetta wide-eyed.

Jacquetta didn't answer. It would take much too long to explain. "What are you doing here yourself?" she asked.

"Feedin' sugar to the horses," the girl said. She looked half frightened, half defiant as she held up a small sack.

"Yes, I know that," Jacquetta said impatiently. "Are Yankees living in the house? When did they come? How long are they staying?" She drew a deep breath and asked the biggest question of all. "Where are my father and mother?"

The girl's face was blank. It was as if she put on a mask, Jacquetta thought, a wooden mask of unknowing. "I just works in the kitchen," she said.

"You were here when the Yankees came, weren't you? You must have heard something!"

"Yes'm," the girl said. "Was a lotta noise."

"But you must hear them talking about their plans."

"Don't no Yankees come in the kitchen," the girl said. "In the kitchen it's just me and Iza."

"You don't spend every waking minute in the kitchen," Jacquetta insisted. "Iza sends you on errands. She sends you out here—"

The girl's mask vanished, and her face shone with amazement. "Sends me! Iza'd never send me with sugar 'less she took sick with the brain fever!"

"Well, what are you doing here, then?" Jacquetta repeated. They seemed to be going round in circles.

There was a glimmer of mischief in the girl's eyes as she repeated, "Feedin' sugar to the horses."

Jacquetta's hip throbbed. She sank onto the bottom rung of the ladder. "Take a look outside," she said. "Is anybody coming?"

The girl went to the door and peered out. "No'm. Cap'n Harris, he be standin' out there by hisself on watch, but he lookin' the other way."

"Captain Harris is the sentry? You know their names, then! How many of them are there?"

"Last night I serves them in the dining-room," the girl said. "There's Colonel Matthews and Major Landor, and Cap'n Harris and Cap'n Ross. Then there's Doc Graham, and all the wounded. Those are Yankees, too, if you want to count them."

"You mean the house is a Yankee hospital?" Jacquetta remembered what the man with the pipe had said about tomorrow: "We'll know how many wounded we've got and we'll know how bad they are."

"They bringin' another wagonload tonight," the girl said, and added, "I heard 'bout that in the dining-room."

"You came to Green Haven last summer, didn't you?" Jacquetta said. "What do they call you?"

"My name is Peace." The girl glanced toward the door and added, "Iza be lookin' for me soon." Of course, Jacquetta thought, Peace ought to go back to the kitchen. But why should she? Mama and Papa weren't there to keep the house running. No one was in charge but the Yankees.

"I be goin' now," Peace said.

Jacquetta felt a rising panic. She still hadn't learned anything about her parents. Peace knew things. Jacquetta needed her help. Somehow she had to win Peace's confidence.

"You know all the horses by name," she said, trying to keep her voice steady. "Do you come every day?"

"Mornin' and night, when I can."

"Do you always bring sugar?"

Peace shook her head. She edged nervously toward the door. "No, Miss Jacquie. I just brung sugar today, just this once."

Peace was skittish as an unbroken colt. The more Jacquetta asked questions, the more she shied away. Jacquetta resolved to find a different approach. The horses, she thought. Through the horses maybe she could gain Peace's trust.

Painfully Jacquetta hoisted herself back to her feet. She limped over to Samoset's stall. The stallion watched her, head high and alert. "Hey, Sam," she said, patting his nose. "Good to see you, fella." She felt Peace's gaze follow her as she moved down the row of stalls, greeting each of the horses in turn. Most of the stalls were empty. Only five mares were in the barn — Tina and Dorcas, Cass, Jilly and Beechnut. It was heartbreaking to touch their familiar faces, to read the trust in their eyes, and to know that tomorrow they, too, would be led away to the war.

"Beechnut, did you get your sugar yet?" She glanced sidelong at Peace, hoping for a reaction.

Peace looked sidelong back. "She say, 'Where mine at?'"

Jacquetta gestured toward the sack in Peace's hand. "Give her some," she said. Peace smiled openly this time, and gave a lump of sugar to Beechnut. Then her face clouded. "They won't be gettin' no sugar treats in the Yankee army," she said with a sigh.

"I wonder why they didn't take these six when they took the rest," Jacquetta mused.

"They rounded up all that was in the fields," Peace said. "The cotton was afire, and the horses was fixin' to make a stampede."

"And they forgot the ones in the barn?" Jacquetta asked.

"Yes'm. Till today."

"I hate to think of it!" Jacquetta burst out. "They're beautiful horses, and gentle! I hate to think what's going to happen to them!"

"They be fine horses all right. Every one of 'em."

"I wish I could save them somehow," Jacquetta said. "I wish I could hide them before the Yankees take them away!"

Peace fell quiet, running her fingers through Beechnut's silvery mane. When she spoke at last she caught Jacquetta by surprise. "Miss Jacquie," she asked, "you hurt your leg?"

"I fell," Jacquetta explained. "Chance threw me when he got a whiff of the smoke. You know Chance?"

"Sure I knows Chance. You done hid him?"

"For now," Jacquetta said. "But it's not a very safe place."

"Where your leg hurt?" Peace asked. When Jacquetta pointed to her hip, Peace clicked her tongue sympathetically. "I'm gonna fetch you something for that," she stated. "You can get up that ladder again? That's good. Stay out of sight and I be comin' right back."

Jacquetta's hip was stiffening up. She couldn't imagine how she'd climbed the apple tree little more than an hour ago.

The world was turned upside down, she thought, as she reached the top of the ladder. She was the young lady of the family, and Peace was a slave from the kitchen. Now she, Jacquetta, was hiding like a rat in the hayloft while Peace skipped off on whatever errand she had invented.

Mama would be horrified if she found out. Jacquetta had always played with the slave children when she was little, but before she went away to Miss Woodworth's Mama said it was time for her to act like a young lady around the servants. Maybe she wouldn't tell Mama about giving treats to the horses with Peace. It would be different with Papa. As soon as she saw him alone she'd tell him the whole story.

Jacquetta thought about how strange and unpredictable life was. As she nestled into the hay, prickles and all, and closed her eyes, she promised herself to try and learn something from this unexpected change of circumstances. In moments she was fast asleep.

"Miss Jacquie?"

Peace's voice pulled Jacquetta back to the world. Her head and arms emerged into the dimness of the loft. Jacquetta sat up hurriedly and ran her fingers through her tangled hair, trying to brush out the bits of hay. "Rub on some of this," Peace said. She held out a little clay pot. It was filled with a gummy, greenish substance that gave off a piny smell.

"What is it?" Jacquetta asked warily.

"Lotta things. Willow bark and sassafras mostly. Rub it into the skin real good."

Peace scrambled the rest of the way up the ladder. She helped Jacquetta unfasten the hooks at the back of her frock. Jacquetta pulled it over her head and tossed it aside gratefully. It was a relief to be rid of all that hot homespun fabric. Pulling up her petticoats, she daubed the gummy salve onto her bruised hip and rubbed it in with her fingertips. Peace looked on approvingly. "I'll leave it here for you," she said. "Any time you start hurtin', just you rub in some more."

"Thank you, Peace," Jacquetta said warmly.

"You hungry?" Peace asked. Jacquetta nodded. Peace reached into her apron pocket and brought out three biscuits, a chicken drumstick and a wedge of cheese, all wrapped in a clean white napkin. She even bounded down the ladder and came back with a pitcher of cool spring water.

"Oh, Peace! This is wonderful!" Jacquetta exclaimed. "Thank you! Thank you!" She was sure food had never tasted so delicious in all her life.

To Jacquetta's relief, Peace stayed in the loft while she ate. Maybe now she could get some answers. She put down the polished chicken bone, drew a deep breath, and began: "Please tell me – what have the Yankees done with my mama and papa?"

"They ain't done nothin' with 'em, Miss Jacquie. Master and Missus run off. The cotton was burnin', the horses was goin' wild, and in all that ruckus Master jump on his mare Ladybird. Happen that Ladybird was ready saddled by the door when the Yankees come. Master puts Missus up in front o' him and off they go." She paused and added with a grin, "That's what we hear 'bout it, out in the kitchen."

"But where are they now?" Jacquetta was almost pleading.

Peace shook her head. "They 'scape from the Yankees. I don't know nothin' more."

"They escaped," Jacquetta repeated. "They're safe!" Something eased inside her, as though a tight knot started to work loose.

"Word is, the Clarences run off, too," Peace said. "Everybody tryin' to get away from the Yankees."

"But where have Mama and Papa gone?" Jacquetta asked. "How am I going to find them?"

Peace shook her head. "I don' know where they be, Miss Jacquie. But people talks. Word go 'round from one plantation to 'nother. Maybe it won' be so long 'fore you hear."

"I hope you're right," Jacquetta sighed. A wave of misery threatened to overwhelm her. She felt utterly helpless. All she could do was wait and hope.

Peace sat back on her heels. She asked a question of her own. "You really mean it, 'bout wantin' to hide the horses?"

Jacquetta looked at her hard. "Of course I do," she said.

"Well then," said Peace, "you can help me an' my brother."

"I didn't know you have a brother!"

"Wit," Peace explained. "He work in the barn."

"Oh, I know Wit!" Jacquetta said. "He's the best groom we've got. But – why do the two of you want to hide the horses?"

Peace hesitated. "They don' harm nobody," she said, struggling for words. "You take care o' them, feed them and talk to them, an' pretty soon you start to love them. None of 'em ought to go to the war. It ain't right!"

Jacquetta listened in amazement. Everything Peace said echoed her own thoughts. "Do you and Wit have a plan?" she asked.

"There's a place he know, in the swamp. We can hide the horses there."

"But how will we get them out of the barn? The sentry will see us."

Peace grinned. "Not if he be lookin' someplace else."

"What do you mean?"

"Tonight when the wagon come in, they'll have their hands full with the wounded men. An' when they be busy with all that, Wit'll give 'em something fresh to worry 'bout. Maybe he gonna see some Rebels on their way here."

"And then..."

"While he off showin' 'em where the Rebels at, you and me hide the horses."

Jacquetta felt her sense of helplessness slip away. She didn't know yet how she would find Mama and Papa, but here was something important that she could do.

In the barn below, a horse nickered softly. A tail swished against the side of a stall. "All right," Jacquetta said. "Let's do it. The Yankees have Green Haven, but they won't get the rest of Papa's horses."

✶ Chapter Five ✶

Jacquetta couldn't remember such a long day in all her life. Sometimes she slept in her nest of hay, and measured the slow progress of the sun each time she woke. Now and then she daubed Peace's mysterious salve onto her hip. The pain receded to a dull ache, only a dim memory of the angry throbbing she had felt before.

When she grew unbearably restless in her hiding-place, Jacquetta climbed into the apple tree to keep a watch on the yard. The soldier with the pipe was on sentry duty now. By catching bits of conversation she learned that he was Major Landor. The Yankee with the red hair was Captain

Ross. They saluted whenever a tall, grey-haired soldier stepped out the back door, and she knew he must be Colonel Matthews. The men complained about the "infernal heat" and praised Iza's cooking. Major Landor said it was a shame such a fine cook had been wasted on a pack of Rebels, and wouldn't he love to take her back to Massachusetts.

Toward late afternoon, Peace returned with a big, broad-shouldered boy. Jacquetta recognized him as the groom called Wit. Wit was even more skittish than Peace. He barely poked his head above the top of the ladder before he disappeared again. "We gonna rope up the horses," Peace explained. She spoke in a whisper, though no one else was within earshot. "When the Yankees all out to the front of the house, you and me take the horses and run for it!"

"Run for it?" Jacquetta repeated dubiously.

"Gotta be quick to steal the horses 'fore the Yankees gets wind of it," Peace explained patiently.

"I'm not a horse thief!" Jacquetta protested. "The Yankees are the thieves. These are my family's horses."

"They won't be seein' it like that," said Peace with a shrug.

Jacquetta's stomach lurched. If they spotted her they'd shoot to kill. She couldn't do this – it was impossible. She would have to abandon the horses. At least Chance was still safe. She could get him from the woods and set out in search of Mama and Papa.

But where would she look for them? How could she hope to travel all alone, with Yankees marauding the country? She needed someone on her side, at least one human being to give her comfort and direction. Right now Peace was the only person who could help her. Mama always said it was "a great uncharted mystery" how the slaves learned what was going on among the Delta plantations. Somehow they always knew what was going on before anyone else found out. Peace could listen and learn and bring news of Mama and Papa. In the meantime, Peace seemed determined to rescue the horses. If she wanted help from Peace, Jacquetta decided, she would have to help Peace with her plan.

Jacquetta sat up straight and drew a deep breath.

"What do I have to do?" she asked.

"When the wagon come with the wounded men, the Yankees gonna have their hands full," Peace said. "Then Wit, he be on lookout, he gonna holler that Rebels be comin' down the road." Peace gave Jacquetta a long, measuring look. "Can you ride Samoset and lead Dorcas and Cass? Sam like them two mares the best."

Jacquetta nodded. She'd only ridden Samoset once. He was a horse who knew his own mind, but the presence of the mares was likely to gentle him. "Who will you ride?" she asked.

Peace looked down at her hands. "I can lead 'em on foot," she said. "Beechnut will follow me, and Tina and Jilly like to follow her."

"Why lead them on foot?" Jacquetta asked. "Why not just—" She stopped, as understanding dawned on her. Peace's work had kept her in the kitchen, plucking chickens and kneading dough. When had she ever had time for learning to ride?

"We have to stop and get Chance," Jacquetta said. But when she explained where she had tied him, Peace shook her head. "It's the other way," she said. "Wit will fetch him."

"Promise?" Jacquetta asked.

Peace nodded, smiling. "Promise," she said.

"Peace," Jacquetta said, "are you really sure you want to do this?"

"When we come here to Green Haven, I 'bout crazy missin' my mama, worryin' what become of her. Every chance I get I goes out to the barn to see Wit. An' I make friends with the horses. Specially Beechnut. She always happy to see me, even when I got nothin' to give her. Seem like the horses save me from losin' my mind." She paused and added in a low voice, "I got to do my part now, to save them."

Jacquetta couldn't find words for an answer. She could only nod, her eyes brimming with tears.

Peace suddenly turned practical. "Wait till you hear lotta hollerin', maybe gunshots," she explained. "Soon's I see it's all clear back here, Miss Jacquie, I'll call you. We rope the horses together and lead 'em out the barn."

"All right," Jacquetta said. "We'll do it. I'll be listening."

Peace scrambled down the ladder into the darkness. Jacquetta heard the restless sounds of the horses below – the whisper of hooves in straw, the munching of hay, a questioning whinny and a friendly answer from down the row of stalls. Did the horses know what was about to happen, Jacquetta wondered? She hardly knew herself.

The sun was sliding down the western sky when Jacquetta heard the distant clatter of hooves and rumble of wagon wheels. She slipped out onto her tree branch but she couldn't see what was going on at the front of the house. She had a sense of bustle and confusion, but not of panic. Red-haired Captain Ross still stood watch.

Then, suddenly, someone shouted. A flurry of commotion erupted out of sight near the drive. Adam's hound, Silver, barked frantically. Captain Ross rushed around the corner of the house, and the yard was empty.

Jacquetta scrambled back into the loft. From somewhere below her, Peace called, "Miss Jacquie! Come on!"

Heart racing, Jacquetta clambered down the ladder and headed for Samoset's stall. The moment she opened the door he stepped out smartly, turning his head to take in everything around him.

He was saddled and ready to go. Peace went to work bringing out Dorcas and Beechnut. Each of the horses trailed a lead rope from its bridle. Jacquetta roped her three together as Peace gathered Beechnut, Jilly and Tina. Jacquetta led Samoset from the barn and the little cavalcade followed. The yard was still empty. Even Silver had disappeared. Jacquetta still heard shouting, but it seemed to come from farther away.

Peace nodded in satisfaction. "They headin' out to chase Rebels for a while," she said quietly. "Wit point them the way."

Samoset was more than a hand taller than Chance, and Jacquetta was grateful for the mounting block that stood in the yard. She put one foot on the block and sprang into the saddle. Picking up the reins she felt Samoset tug impatiently. The mares held back, keeping a respectful distance from the stallion. "This way," said Peace, raising her arm. "Hurry!"

As they crossed the yard and entered the woods, Jacquetta felt strangely calm. There was something familiar now about slipping away under cover of darkness. For the second night in a row she fled on horseback, listening for pursuers as she headed for safety. But last night she had only been escaping Uncle Silas and Aunt Clem. This time she fled from the Yankees. If they caught her, they would have no mercy.

Because Peace was on foot, leading her three mares, she tended to trail behind. Jacquetta reined in Samoset to let her catch up. "This way," Peace said, pointing off to the right. "There ain't no path."

Chance would have obeyed in an instant, but at first Samoset fought when Jacquetta tried to turn him off the trail. She gave the reins a sharp tug and nudged him with her heel, clicking encouragement with her tongue. When he finally set off overland, he turned his head frequently, checking to make sure the mares were following. The horses picked their way carefully through the underbrush, weaving between tree trunks. Leafy branches swished along their flanks. Jacquetta dismounted and walked beside Peace, each of them leading their horses through the tangles as best they could.

Time lost all meaning. Jacquetta had no idea

how long they had been winding their way forward. As though they had a life of their own, rocks leaped up to trip her. Fallen branches clawed at her ankles. Mosquitoes whined around her ears. She tried to swat them away with one hand while she held Samoset's reins with the other. The clouds of insects only grew thicker. Underfoot, the ground became spongy. It sucked at her shoes with every step. The air had a damp, fishy smell. Lacy skeins of Spanish moss draped the trees. From all around them sounded a chorus of frogs.

"Watch out for water moccasins," Peace said over the rising din. Jacquetta shuddered. She could barely see her own feet in the moonlight. How could she keep a watch for poisonous snakes?

Samoset snorted and shook his head, making his bridle jingle. He must wonder if they'd gone crazy, Jacquetta thought. Why should he follow this pair of humans who were leading him and his mares into the swamp, farther and farther from their comfortable stable? Why didn't he break away and bolt back to Green Haven? There was only one answer, Jacquetta knew. Samoset and the others had been trained with care. From the time they were foaled, they learned to trust human beings. Through one painstaking lesson after another they had been taught to obey human commands.

"Not much farther now," Peace said as they splashed across a stream.

"I hope not," said Jacquetta, slapping at her forehead. "If the Yankees don't kill us the mosquitoes will!"

"The Yankees can't track us here," Peace said. "The water washes away our prints. Dogs can't even sniff us out."

How did Peace and Wit know so much about tracking and dogs? Why had Wit been to this swampy hiding-place before? Somehow she felt it was best not to ask questions, but she went on wondering.

"We can't leave the horses on wet ground like this!" she told Peace anxiously. "Their hooves will rot."

Peace didn't reply. She simply forged ahead, the horses splashing behind her. Jacquetta struggled to keep up. Her mud-spattered skirts dragged around her legs, and her hip began to ache again.

Nothing seemed to bother Peace. She never

slowed or wavered, but led the way through the swamp as though she followed an invisible road. Staggering after her, Jacquetta was ready to call a halt when Peace cried, "Here it is!"

The underbrush thinned, the ground rose, and suddenly, almost miraculously, they stood in a dry, grassy clearing ringed with trees. A fresh breeze chased away the clinging dampness. Jacquetta felt as though they had emerged from a nightmare and stepped into paradise.

"This is beautiful!" she exclaimed. "It's perfect!"

"It'll be good for the horses," Peace said. "Best place I know for them to hide in."

They didn't talk much as they unfastened the horses from one another and tied them to trees at the meadow's edge. Jacquetta removed Samoset's saddle and hung it over a tree limb. She tried to lean against his shoulder, but he stepped away haughtily to crop the grass. Chance never behaved that way. He always made her welcome.

A storm of questions pounded her brain as soon as she stood still. Would Wit come with news of Mama and Papa? What should she do with the horses when she went to find them? Were Aunt

Clem, Uncle Silas and Cousin Mattie still safe at Brookmoor? Would Wit really bring Chance to the hiding-place? She was too exhausted to think, but the questions kept coming, thick and fast as swamp mosquitoes.

Dawn streaked the sky, and the first sleepy birds began to stir and trill. The girls gathered leaves and branches to make rough beds on the ground. Jacquetta was so tired she thought she'd have been happy to lie down on a bare slab of granite. She closed her eyes and listened to the sighing of the trees overhead, the soft munching of the horses as they grazed, and the rustling of leaves as Peace settled onto her own bed nearby. By the time the sun rose, she was asleep.

✳ Chapter Six ✳

A clear, familiar neigh tore across Jacquetta's dreams. She bolted upright, pushing sleep away from her. There it was again – Chance's neigh! She'd recognize it anywhere.

Jacquetta scrambled up and bounded across the clearing as Wit slid from the saddle. Chance trotted to meet her, whinnying his greeting. His legs and belly were caked with mud, but to Jacquetta the bay gelding was more beautiful than ever. She flung her arms around his neck and hugged him tight.

Peace and Wit were talking earnestly a few yards away. At last Peace turned to Jacquetta. "Miss

Jacquie," she said, "Wit been talking to some of the people from the Clarence place. They says Miss Rachel at Deerfield – that's the Willard plantation – got word 'bout your papa and mama."

"Deerfield!" Jacquetta exclaimed. "Let's go, then! Wit, do you know the way from here?"

Wit nodded shyly. "I'll 'splain the way," he said. "You'll find it fine."

"No, come with me," Jacquetta said. "It'll be better if you show me."

"The Yankees be needin' Wit back at Green Haven," Peace put in. "He have to go back."

"Don't listen to orders from the Yankees!" Jacquetta protested. "They're the enemy!" She jolted to a stop. The Yankees weren't enemies to Peace and Wit. The Yankees had come to set them free.

Wit shifted restlessly from foot to foot, eager to be off. Until now Jacquetta had believed he was unshakeably loyal to her and the whole Logan family. He had gone to great lengths to save the Logan horses – that had seemed all the proof she needed. But now it was clear that he wanted to go back and help the Yankees. By law he and Peace were Logan property, and it made no difference what they wanted to do. But no one was left to enforce the laws they had once lived by, now that the Yankees had taken over.

Jacquetta felt a surge of fear. Maybe Peace would go back, too. Maybe both of them meant to leave her here, and she would have to find her way out of the swamp alone.

"Peace," she said, fighting to keep her voice steady, "will you go to the Willard place with me? Please?"

"I'll go," Peace said. She sounded strong and certain. She wasn't obeying an order. She had made up her own mind.

"It ain't far," Wit assured her. "You see that big cypress? You head that way, out the swamp. Keep to the woods. There's a path most the way. At the fork you goes left to the Willard cotton fields."

"Thank you," Jacquetta said fervently.

Wit handed her Chance's reins. "He's a good horse," he told her. "He act like he know I'm takin' him to you."

"Thank you for bringing him," Jacquetta said. "And for distracting the Yankees. For everything."

When Wit grinned he didn't look skittish at all. "You're most welcome, Miss Jacquie," he said. He hugged Peace goodbye and disappeared into the swamp.

"He brought us vittles," Peace said happily, unfastening Chance's saddlebag. It was packed with more food than Jacquetta could let herself believe in – salt pork, cornbread, fruit preserves, carrots and greens. There were even two slices of pie on one of Mama's bone china plates, carefully wrapped in a cloth.

"This have to last a while," Peace warned as they dug in. "Best we eat just a little at a time."

"Chance should rest a while," Jacquetta said, slicing off a chunk of cornbread. "As soon as he's ready, let's head for Deerfield." She stopped, pondering. Peace didn't know how to ride horseback. She would have to walk, or maybe ride double with Jacquetta on Chance. Unless...

"Peace," she asked, "would you like to learn to ride?"

Peace cast a longing gaze at the horses grazing contentedly in the meadow. "Oh, Miss Jacquie, you think I could?"

"Sure!" Jacquetta said, springing to her feet. "Come on!"

Peace was especially fond of the roan mare Beechnut, so Jacquetta decided Beechnut would be her first mount. She put a folded shawl and Samoset's saddle on Beechnut's back. The saddle was too large for the slender mare, but Jacquetta showed Peace how to cinch up the girth until it fit snugly. A stump served as a mounting block. Peace swung into the saddle and sat still, her eyes wide with amazement. "It's so high up!" she exclaimed. "Seem like halfway to the sky!"

Jacquetta bent and adjusted the stirrups. Beechnut looked over her shoulder questioningly and pawed the ground. She sensed that something unusual was going on, and she wasn't sure she approved. "Hold the reins like this," Jacquetta said. "Now let up on them just a little. There! Nudge her lightly with your heels, and—"

She had no time to say more. Peace gave Beechnut a sharp kick and the mare took off at a run. Galloping full tilt, she circled the field. Then, as though showing off for the rest of the horses, she rose up on her hind legs and gave a vigorous shake. Kicking and shrieking, Peace slid over Beechnut's rump and sprawled to the ground. Beechnut settled on all fours again and bent to take a mouthful of grass as if nothing had happened.

Peace sat up, laughing and unhurt. "Sure is a long way down!" she said. "Ol' Beechnut say, 'Just bring me sugar and stay off o' my back!'"

"She's teasing you," Jacquetta said. "You told her to giddap, so she said, 'All right, off we go!'"

"Maybe I give her too hard a nudge," Peace mused. "What you think, Miss Jacquie?"

"Let's try it on a lead," Jacquetta said. "We should have done that in the first place."

Peace got up, brushed herself off, and picked up Beechnut's trailing reins. "Come here, you," she said, leading her back to the stump. "No more o' your tricks now."

Beechnut stood patiently as Peace remounted. Jacquetta found a rope to serve as a leading rein for Beechnut, and held onto it as she mounted Chance and moved slightly ahead. For a moment both girls sat still.

Beechnut gave a playful whinny and danced her

forefeet up and down. "Make her stop that," Jacquetta counselled. "That's it — keep the reins tight. Show her you're the boss. Now, just a gentle nudge... there you go..."

Peace's heels barely touched Beechnut's flanks this time. The mare set off at a sedate walk. Jacquetta held Chance to the same gentle pace, keeping a slight lead. "A little faster?" Jacquetta asked when they had gone once around the meadow.

"Faster!" Peace called excitedly.

Jacquetta clicked her tongue and gave Chance another nudge. He shifted his pace to a brisk trot. Beechnut broke into a trot as well. Startled and half afraid, Peace grabbed a handful of mane and struggled to stay in the saddle.

"You've got to post!" Jacquetta cried. "Rise up and sit down."

"I can't!" Peace yelled. "She's gonna bounce me right off her!"

Jacquetta slowed Chance's pace a little, and Beechnut slowed, too. Peace began to sense Beechnut's rhythm, rising and settling with the mare's movements.

"You've got it!" Jacquetta told her. "You're posting!"

"This as fast as I wanta go," Peace said. "I thought she 'bout to rattle me to pieces!"

"You'll like going fast after a while," Jacquetta assured her. "You'll see."

They made another trip around the clearing and drew the horses to a halt. Peace looked extremely pleased with herself. "I always wished I could learn to ride, but I never thought I'd get a chance," she said, beaming. "Thank you, Miss Jacquie!"

"That was beautiful!" Jacquetta exclaimed. "Looks like you were born to it!"

Peace slid to the ground and patted Beechnut happily. "My mama always say I born to be special," she said. "I wish she coulda seen me just now."

Peace's smile faded. She seemed suddenly far away.

Jacquetta wanted to call her back. "Special?" she repeated. "Special how?"

Peace shook her head. "Special what Mama want for me, an' Wit, too. That how come she got us Bible names."

"What do you mean?" Jacquetta asked.

"When I born, Mama ask the mistress to choose for me. The mistress close her eyes and open the Bible. She put her finger on the words, and then she open her eyes to read. 'Depart from evil, and do good; seek peace, and pursue it.'"

"'Seek peace, and pursue it,'" Jacquetta murmured. In the quiet of the clearing the words seemed to ring out, brave and clear.

"Wit come from the Bible, too. His name Witness. 'This stone shall be a witness unto us; for it hath heard all the words of the Lord.'"

Jacquetta felt the pride in Peace's voice. She thought of Peace's mother, finding a way to give her children an enduring gift.

There were more than sixty slaves at Green Haven, and Jacquetta realized she had never thought much about their lives and their feelings. Now she and Peace were working and playing together as if they were equals. It felt almost as though they were friends.

What would Mama say if she could see Jacquetta now, teaching Peace to ride? "Treat the servants kindly," Mama always told her, "but never let them get above their station. Make sure they always know their proper place." Well, there was no proper place out here in the swamp meadow – not for her or for Peace. If it weren't for the colour of their skins, no one could tell which one was the mistress and which the servant.

Servant. The word caught somewhere in Jacquetta's mind and turned itself over and over. Servant – that was what everyone called the dark-skinned people who worked in the fields and the stables, who swept the floors and cooked the meals and emptied the chamber pots. But real servants were paid for their labour. Real servants were free to go and look for other work if they weren't happy, taking their families with them. Peace and Wit and the dozens of others at Green Haven weren't servants. They were slaves. Jacquetta had known it all her life, of course, but she had learned to step politely around the fact. Slavery was part of life, but nice people didn't dwell on it.

But the Yankees were forcing people to think about slavery, and talk about it, and fight for it in this terrible war. A bunch of Yankees up north said all the slaves should be set free, to come and go as they pleased. "Suppose they're right," Marcus had said to Papa one night after dinner. "Do you think slavery will come to an end some day?"

"I doubt it," Papa had told him. "We need workers to raise our crops, and the slaves need to be cared for. They're not equipped to survive on their own."

Jacquetta watched Peace as she combed the tangles out of Beechnut's mane with her fingers. She, Jacquetta, was the one ill-equipped to survive on her own. If it weren't for Peace, the Yankees would have caught her by now, and stolen every last one of the Logan Morgans.

Suddenly she wanted to know this girl who had become so important in her life. She wanted to know where Peace had come from, what she loved and what she hated, what she thought about when she was alone. She didn't know how to begin.

"Where did you live before you came to Green Haven?" Jacquetta asked.

"We growed up on a plantation near Tupelo," Peace said. "The master died two years back, and his son sold everybody off."

"And your mama—"

Peace looked at the ground. "They sold her down the river to New Orleans."

Jacquetta knew that every slave dreaded being sold down the river. The slave market at New Orleans was infamous. It was a place where buyers traded in human beings as though they were horses or cattle. What must it be like, Jacquetta wondered, to know that your own mother had been taken to such a place and auctioned off to the highest bidder?

Peace turned away, changing the subject abruptly. "Think Beechnut gonna let me ride her over to Deerfield?" she asked.

"Sure she will," Jacquetta told her. "You've got her respect now."

They started for Deerfield in mid-afternoon, riding Chance and Beechnut and leaving the rest of the horses in the clearing. Jacquetta kept Beechnut on a lead and tried to hold a pace that Peace could manage. The farther they went, the more confident Peace seemed to become.

For a few frantic minutes when they emerged from the swamp they couldn't find the path Wit had promised. Then, suddenly, it opened before them as if by magic. The path was narrow and looked as though it wasn't often used. Just as well, Jacquetta thought. Maybe the Yankees knew nothing about it.

Jacquetta had only been to the Willard place once before. She and Mama had attended a party and been guests at the big house for three days. Jacquetta remembered Lucinda Willard, a pretty, lively girl a year older than Cousin Mattie. As she and Peace rode along, Jacquetta let herself imagine that they were off to pay Lucinda Willard a visit. They'd eat pretty iced cakes on the veranda, and Lucinda would show them her new brocade gown, and a filigree brooch her papa had brought her from New Orleans...

Jacquetta shook her head and pulled herself back to reality. She was filthy and bedraggled, her dress torn, her clothes caked with mud. She was riding beside a slave girl who had become her only friend. There was a Yankee hospital at Green Haven, and Yankees were spreading themselves all over the Delta. Whatever they found at Deerfield, it wouldn't be a party.

✳ Chapter Seven ✳

Even before Deerfield came into view, Jacquetta saw that the family was gone. It was late afternoon, and the fields should have bustled with workers as they finished the day's hoeing and weeding. Instead the cotton stood untended, as though no one was in charge any longer. From somewhere floated the cheerful notes of a banjo. It seemed the workers had declared a holiday.

"Wait here," Peace told her. She dismounted, passed Beechnut's reins to Jacquetta, and disappeared among the trees. The banjo grew louder. Voices broke into song: "Jimmy crack corn, but I don't care. Ol' master's gone away..."

Jacquetta paced uneasily back and forth. She wondered who Peace was talking to, and what she was saying. At last the music stopped abruptly. "Come on, Miss Jacquie," Peace called. Her voice was full of excitement.

"I'm coming," Jacquetta called back, and heard the wariness in her own voice. Carefully she tied the horses, stalling for time, half afraid of what she would find. She had to talk to someone called Rachel, she reminded herself. Rachel could tell her about Papa and Mama.

The Willard house was smaller than the house at Green Haven, its yard edged with flower gardens. The roses were in full bloom, and their fragrance wafted on the breeze. The yard was filled with people. Black people. Some wore the usual homespun servants' clothes, but others were dressed in finery, as though they had raided the family's wardrobes. A very tall young man in a silk shirt and pleated trousers stepped forward, holding out his hand. "Good day to you," he said with a mocking smile. "You must be Miss Jacquie that Peace been tellin' us about."

Jacquetta glanced at Peace for help. Peace smiled

back reassuringly. "I came to see Rachel," Jacquetta explained. "Is she here?"

"Perhaps she is," the tall boy said. "Or perhaps she ain't."

"Oh, Samson, don't torment the young lady!" A withered old woman hobbled out of the crowd, her skin the colour of dark honey. She held out a gnarled hand to Jacquetta. "I'm Miss Rachel," she said. "Don't let him frighten you."

Jacquetta took the woman's hand. Something in her presence seemed to radiate kindness. Jacquetta wondered what she should call her. Since she was a slave, it ought to be Rachel without the "Miss". But that didn't feel right. The old woman had so much dignity she could only be called Miss Rachel.

"Peace's brother Wit says you have word of my mother and father, Miss Rachel," Jacquetta said. "Roger and Elvira Logan from Green Haven."

Miss Rachel nodded. "Look like you could use a wash and some clean clothes," she stated. "Come inside and freshen up. I'll tell you all I know."

Jacquetta glanced back at Peace as she followed Miss Rachel into the house. Peace was deep in conversation with two girls about her own age, and made no move to go with her.

"Where are the Willards?" Jacquetta asked as Miss Rachel led her upstairs.

"They got word the Yankees was comin' and off they run," Miss Rachel said. "Only no Yankees ain't come yet. The house be left to us coloured. This here Miss Lucinda's dressing room. Leave your muddy things and put on somethin' of hers."

For a few moments Jacquetta couldn't bring herself to open Lucinda's wardrobe. It felt more than strange to be in someone else's dressing room, ready to make off with things that didn't belong to her. But the thought of clean, dry clothes was irresistible. Soon she was poring over Lucinda's frocks and gowns, trying to make up her mind. She chose the simplest frock she could find, and a crisp taffeta petticoat to wear underneath it. Miss Rachel brought a pitcher of fresh water for the washstand. She even found Jacquetta a brush and a neatly pressed ribbon for her hair. Jacquetta looked in the mirror and smiled at herself in delight.

"Now, let me tell you about your people," Miss

Rachel said, settling into an armchair. "Day 'fore yesterday I was down at the Clarence place, nursing little Ella. She's a sickly child, and she took bad with the croup. I knows a bit 'bout tendin' sick chillun, so Miss Clarence sent over for me.

"Little Ella was much better in the mornin' and I was fixin' to come back to Deerfield, when there break out a powerful lot o' shoutin' and shootin' from over at Green Haven. The Yankees done come, ridin' down from Vicksburg. Some of 'em set your papa's cotton on fire. Some others of 'em put it out 'fore it spread. What a ruckus and commotion! In all the smoke and the noise, your papa and mama ride horseback up to the Clarence place, hollerin' for help. But John Clarence and the boys is all off to the war, and it's no one there but the womenfolk and the little one. They all pile into a wagon, with a few clothes and some china and such, and they head on down the road. Your mama and papa, and Miss Clarence and her old mama, and little Ella just up from her sickbed. Headin' south, all of them. I hear your papa say, 'We'll go to James in Alexandria.'"

"James – that's my uncle," Jacquetta said. "One

of Papa's brothers. Alexandria's in Louisiana."

"Across the big river," Miss Rachel said, shaking her head. "I don't know how they're likely to cross."

"Maybe I can catch up with them before they get there," Jacquetta said. "I should leave here right away."

Miss Rachel frowned. "Ain't safe for a young lady alone," she said. "Let me think who can go with you."

Somewhere in the distance came voices and the sound of tramping feet. As the noise drew closer, Jacquetta and Miss Rachel hurried to the window. Half a dozen grey-clad Confederate soldiers were passing down the road. Jacquetta was about to wave to them when someone gave a shout. The roar of a rifle ripped the summer air. She glimpsed two figures in blue at the edge of the woods. One of them had fired on the Rebel troops.

From the window Jacquetta couldn't follow what happened next. Through the smoke of rifle fire she saw a tangled knot of men, some in grey and some in blue. More shots rang out. Someone screamed. There was another shot, a cry of agony, and the knot tore apart and scattered into the distance. In moments it was over save for a haze of smoke and the frantic barking of dogs. The two men in blue uniforms lay motionless in the road.

Jacquetta sank to the floor and covered her face with her hands. A wail of terror burst from her throat. Then she was sobbing, her body shaking beyond her control. All of the fears she had fought since Uncle Silas brought news of Vicksburg, all the pictures of destruction she had tried to keep from her mind, overcame her in those swift moments of violence. The war was real. It was murderous and inescapable. Without warning it had shown her its senseless fury.

"There, there," Miss Rachel murmured, gathering Jacquetta into her arms. "They's all gone now. Nothin' gonna harm you." But Jacquetta went on crying. She cried for the men and horses slaughtered at Vicksburg, for the fields burned, for the people driven from their homes, for families splintered like firewood. She cried for Marcus and Adam, and not knowing whether they were alive or dead. She cried for Mama and Papa, struggling to make their way to Alexandria through country mad with fighting.

After a while Miss Rachel led Jacquetta into Lucinda's bedchamber. She settled her beneath the canopy of the big four-poster bed. Exhausted, Jacquetta fell into a deep sleep.

"Miss Jacquie? Miss Jacquie! Wake up!"

Jacquetta sat up and rubbed the sleep from her eyes. For a few seconds she struggled to remember where she was. Then it all flooded back to her – Miss Rachel's story, the shots in the road. Through the window she saw that the sun was about to set, and knew she hadn't slept long.

Peace stood beside the bed, peering in through the curtains. "Miss Jacquie, they done killed a Yankee and wounded another one. Look like he fixin' to die, too."

"Where is he?" Jacquetta asked.

"Down in the parlour. Miss Rachel be nursin' him. He's hurt bad."

Jacquetta shuddered. While she lay on a flowered counterpane surrounded by lace curtains, a man was dying in this very house. But why should she care if a Yankee died, she asked herself.

Nobody had invited them to Mississippi. They'd whipped up this war themselves. Now they'd have to pay the price.

"Miss Rachel askin' for you to come down," Peace was saying. "He got a paper on him. With writin' on it."

"She wants me to read it?" Jacquetta asked.

Peace nodded. Peace couldn't read. Neither, it seemed, could Miss Rachel or any of the other slaves on the Willard place. Jacquetta was the only person in the house who could unlock the mysteries of the wounded Yankee's paper.

The injured man lay on a settee in the parlour. When Peace and Jacquetta came in, Miss Rachel was washing a wound along his temple. She had wrapped strips of cloth around his right arm and his left leg to serve as bandages, but already crimson smears of blood had begun to seep through. Several of the women Jacquetta had seen in the yard hovered in the room, trying to help. One stirred up a feeble breeze with a lacquered fan. Another washed the soldier's blistered feet.

The man had light-brown hair and a smooth, boyish face. His eyes were closed. Jacquetta thought he might be dead already, until he gave a low moan. "Is he conscious?" she whispered.

Miss Rachel shook her head. "He don't feel nothin' right now," she whispered back. "When he wake up he gonna have pain."

"Is there something you can give him?"

"Master Willard's brandy is all. If we had a doctor, he could have one of them pain powders."

"Where that paper, Miss Rachel?" Peace asked. "Let Miss Jacquie see it."

Miss Rachel handed Jacquetta a crumpled envelope. Jacquetta pulled out a letter, written in a neat, even hand.

"Dear Mama, Papa, Kip and Katie," she read aloud. "I know it's been an awfully long time since you've heard from me. I think of you every day, but we're on the move so much I don't have time to write. I guess you read in the papers about Vicksburg. Thank God the worst was over by the time my unit got there. I'll have nightmares all my life about some of the things I saw. Sometimes it helps if I close my eyes and think about ordinary things like helping in the store and sitting through church service, building the tree house with Kip and riding with Katie out to the falls."

Jacquetta paused. Tears blurred her vision. She struggled to read through the tightness in her throat. "I keep hoping this war will be over soon and they'll let us go home. I miss you all and love you more than I can tell you. Jim."

"Didn't she read that out pretty!" exclaimed the woman with the fan.

"She went to school all the way in Virginia," Peace said proudly.

"Well then!" said the one with the fan. "No wonder!"

Jacquetta folded the letter into its envelope and handed it back to Miss Rachel. "If he wakes up," she said, "maybe he'll tell us where to send it."

She looked down at the Yankee soldier's face again. He might be eighteen or a little older – about the same age as her own brother Marcus. He had a brother and sister. It sounded as though his father ran a store somewhere up north.

And he had a name. He was called Jim.

Maybe Adam or Marcus, or both of them, lay wounded somewhere at this very moment, Jacquetta thought as she gazed down at Jim. If she helped Jim, maybe someone would help her brothers, too, wherever they were. She didn't know what she could do, but there must be something. Once she helped Jim she would be ready to search for Mama and Papa.

If only they had left her a letter, some set of instructions to guide her on her way. Perhaps they tried to send word to Brookmoor, thinking she was still safe with Uncle Silas and Aunt Clem. They had no idea she was here at Deerfield. But she had news of them now. Somehow she had to find her way across the Mississippi to Alexandria.

✳ Chapter Eight ✳

Jacquetta knew that the sooner she got started, the better her chances were of catching up with Papa and Mama. But the thought of setting out for Alexandria was daunting. She would have to venture into country where she had never travelled before. And what should she do about the horses? She couldn't abandon them in the clearing. She wanted to bring them safely to Papa. They would be the foundation of a new Logan line. But how could she take them all the way to Louisiana, across the Mississippi? How would she cross the river herself?

As desperately as she wanted to hurry, she

needed time to think. She had to gather information and form a plan.

After a while Jacquetta went out and found Peace in the yard, laughing with some of her new friends. "Let's bring in the horses," Jacquetta told her. "They deserve a good rub-down and some proper feed."

The Willards had taken their horses with them when they'd fled. The stable was empty, so Chance and Beechnut got the two biggest stalls. Jacquetta curried Chance until every fleck of mud was gone, and his reddish-brown coat glistened. Peace worked on Beechnut as though she were an artist completing a painting. The girls left the horses munching fresh bales of hay and went inside to check on Jim.

He had just awakened when they returned to the parlour. His eyes were open, and he stirred restlessly on the settee. Jacquetta strained to catch his thin, cracked words. "Ma?" he murmured. "What happened?"

"You're safe with us," Miss Rachel told him. "Lie still now. Lie easy."

Later Jacquetta stopped Miss Rachel as she

headed out to the kitchen. "Is he going to be all right now?" she asked.

Miss Rachel sighed. "I don't like the looks of that arm of his. It's swole up pretty bad. There's a bullet lodged somewhere, and we got no way to get it out."

"But he's awake," Jacquetta insisted. "That must mean he's getting better, doesn't it?"

"He don't know where he is nor who he is," Miss Rachel said sadly. "If he takes a fever we could lose him."

A cold finger of dread slithered down Jacquetta's spine. They couldn't let him die, she thought desperately. It didn't matter that he was a Yankee. He was a boy like her own brothers. He liked to ride with his sister out to the falls. He wanted to go home.

"Maybe it'd help if a doctor took care of him," Jacquetta said. "There's a hospital at Green Haven. A Yankee hospital."

Miss Rachel picked up a little brass candlestick from the sideboard. She turned it thoughtfully in her hands. "It'd be a danger to move him. But could be a greater danger to keep him here."

"Did the Willards leave a wagon?" Jacquetta asked. "We could lay him in a wagon with pillows and blankets and find the smoothest way to take him."

"We'll see," Miss Rachel said. "We'll see how he looks in the morning."

That night Jacquetta slept in Lucinda's bed, surrounded by the sounds of people coming and going. With the Willard family gone the slaves had taken over the whole house. They shouted to one another from the attic to the cellars. They laughed on the stairs and pounded on the piano in the drawing room. Some of the men broke into Mr Willard's store of wine. Their drunken voices rose and fell.

When the noise grew too loud Miss Rachel ordered them to hush, and reminded them that the wounded Yankee was trying to rest. After all, Jacquetta heard her explain, he was their honoured guest, fighting far from his home so that some day they could all be free. A respectful quiet fell over the house for a little while, but soon the noise rose again. Every quarter hour the grandfather clock chimed, a lonesome reminder of the order that was gone.

Jacquetta pulled a pillow over her head, but the noise found its way to her all the same. The slaves had tossed aside patience, obedience and respect for their masters. They acted as if the Willards had gone forever, leaving the whole plantation in their hands. She *had* come to a party, Jacquetta thought, but not the sort she could ever have imagined.

She tried to think about the journey ahead of her, but she couldn't concentrate. It wasn't only the noise that troubled her, it was the strangeness. She felt as though she had wandered into a world where she didn't belong, and she had no idea how to find her way out again. Even Peace had deserted her. She was enjoying the party, having fun with her new friends, while Jacquetta worried upstairs alone.

From somewhere a woman began to sing. Her voice was unpolished, but there was passion in her song. Other voices joined in. Hands clapped and feet stamped the floor. Jacquetta slipped out of bed and crept to the top of the stairs to listen. "Go down, Moses!" they sang, "Way down in Egypt land! Tell ol' Pharaoh, let my people go!"

Peering over the banister, Jacquetta saw the hallway crowded with people, singing and swaying to the music. Peace stood near the foot of the stairs. Her face shone with excitement.

Jacquetta closed her eyes and tried to imagine how she would feel if she had been a slave all her life. Would she be overjoyed at this sudden taste of freedom? Would she find herself seething with fury at the people who had for so long been her masters? Maybe she'd join the party in the house. Perhaps she'd sample fine foods for the first time, and eat off the best china. Maybe she'd put on the mistress's silk gowns and dainty shoes, and sit in the drawing room as if she were gentry. Surely she would lift her voice in that passionate refrain: "Let my people go!"

Actually, Jacquetta reflected, the Willard slaves were far more well-behaved than she herself might have been if the tables were turned. Maybe it was Miss Rachel's influence. Miss Rachel had kindness, and wisdom too. When help was needed, she knew exactly what to do. She didn't seem to care that Jacquetta came from a slave-owning family. She saw her weariness, her loneliness and her fear, and treated her as a fellow human being in need. Miss Rachel was a lady in the very truest sense.

Then there was Peace. Peace had been helping her almost from the moment they met. How could she begrudge Peace a bit of fun now, after her year working in the Logan kitchen and her mother sold down the river?

The singers burst into another chorus. Jacquetta tiptoed back to Lucinda's room and climbed into the big canopy bed again. The strains of "Go Down, Moses" lulled her to sleep.

"How is Jim today?" Jacquetta asked when she saw Miss Rachel outside the parlour the next morning.

"Clear in his head, but more feverish than yesterday," Miss Rachel said. "I tol' him 'bout Green Haven and he say he want to go."

Jacquetta drew a deep breath. "We could hitch Chance and Beechnut to the Willards' wagon," she said. "I can take him to Green Haven if you think he can stand the trip."

"Ain't nothin' more we can do for him," Miss

Rachel said, shaking her head. "He won' las' no way if he stay here."

Jacquetta struggled with a tangle of thoughts and emotions. She had offered to take Jim to the Yankee hospital, and she was happy that she might be able to help him. But this detour would delay her search for Mama and Papa. Besides, it made no sense to take Chance and Beechnut back to Green Haven. She had worked so hard to keep them out of Yankee hands, and now they would be in danger all over again. Part of her wished she hadn't spoken up to Miss Rachel at all.

Then she thought of her brothers. She pictured Adam, with his gap-toothed grin and sparkling blue eyes, always daring her to some new feat of courage. She thought of Marcus, quiet and serious, "steady as the day is long", as Papa liked to say. Once, when she was ten, she'd stepped on a yellowjackets' nest and run screaming to the house, covered with stings. It was Marcus who carried her to the creek and wrapped her in mud packs, Marcus who calmed her with his voice and his gentleness.

She couldn't start for Alexandria until she had

done whatever she could for Jim. She had made a bargain with fate, and she had to keep her promise.

"Can Chance and Beechnut pull a wagon?" Peace asked anxiously, coming up beside her. "I thought they was just for saddle."

"They can pull in harness too," Jacquetta assured her. "They're Morgans. Morgans can do anything!"

"I'll tell some of the men to get the wagon ready," Miss Rachel said. "One of them can go with you for protection on the road."

"Oh, I'll be all right," Jacquetta began, but Miss Rachel gave a disapproving snort and hurried off.

Jacquetta turned back to Peace. "Will you come with me back to Green Haven?" she asked hopefully.

Peace nodded. "I needs to see Wit," she said. "Have to talk to him 'bout somethin'." She hesitated and went on, "Maybe me and Wit can go and look for our mama, like you lookin' for yours."

Jacquetta stared at her in amazement. "In New Orleans?" she exclaimed.

"That's where they was takin' her," Peace said.

"That's where we have to start lookin'."

It would be almost impossible, Jacquetta thought, but she didn't want to crush Peace's hopes. "You'll come with me then," she said. "Let's get the horses ready."

Under Miss Rachel's careful direction, three of the men carried Jim on his mattress out to the Willards' wagon, which stood in the yard. Jim kept trying to sit up, but Miss Rachel told him to stay quiet. Jacquetta hitched up the horses, who snorted and stamped, eager to be off. She was about to climb onto the driver's seat when Samson, the slave who had mocked her when she'd arrived at Deerfield, stepped in front of her.

"I'm gonna go with you to that Yankee hospital," he announced. "I'm gonna see those Yankees over there and join the Yankee army. Meantime I'll be your escort."

Jacquetta appealed to Miss Rachel. "We'll be fine by ourselves," she insisted.

Miss Rachel wouldn't hear of it. "No tellin' what might happen on the road," she said. She gave Samson a long hard look and added, "I'm trustin' you to take good care of everyone, you unnerstand?"

"Yes'm," Samson said solemnly. He sounded as though he meant it. "I'll drive the wagon," he told Jacquetta. "I been Master Willard's coachman."

Jacquetta opened her mouth to argue, but Peace called to her from the bed of the wagon. "Sit back here with me," she said. "You can help me case Jim need anythin'."

Jacquetta climbed into the wagon and settled herself beside Peace in a nest of cushions. Jim seemed to be asleep, his wounded arm propped on pillows. Samson flicked his whip lightly across the horses' rumps, and they were off.

Samson knew all the roads to Green Haven. He drove fearlessly, as though they had every right to travel in the open. "What'll we do if we run into a pack of Yankees?" Jacquetta whispered to Peace.

"Ask 'em to lead us the way, how 'bout?" Peace said, laughing.

Jacquetta tried to imagine how she would explain herself to a Yankee patrol. Here they were, two slaves and a Rebel girl, taking a wounded Yankee to a Yankee hospital. Maybe she could leave the patrol so befuddled that he'd let them pass. But still, there were the horses. Any good Yankee soldier would commandeer them straight away.

"We can't just ride up to the big house, you know," Jacquetta told Peace, trying to keep her voice low. "We'll have to watch out for the sentry." She tried to think as the wagon creaked and jolted along the road. "We'll stop and unhitch the horses before we get to the drive. We can hide Chance and Beechnut in the woods."

"We can't just leave Mr Jim all alone, waitin' to be found," Peace pointed out.

"I know," Jacquetta said. "You go up to the house and explain everything to Wit. He can tell the Yankees to bring in a wounded soldier."

Peace shook her head doubtfully. "It might work," she said.

"It's got to work!" Jacquetta insisted. "It's the only way to save the horses. What else can we do?"

"Hope for good luck," Peace said simply.

They were coming to a crossing, an old wooden bridge over a wide stream. "Chance is a little afraid of bridges," Jacquetta told Samson. "Let him take a good look at it first."

Samson didn't answer. He cast her a sullen glance and urged the team forward. Chance tested the bridge with a careful hoof. Beechnut stopped too, waiting for Chance to let her know that it was safe to move forward. The wagon stood still. Impatiently Samson snapped the whip across Chance's back. Chance flung up his head and neighed indignantly.

"No!" Jacquetta cried. "Don't hit him! Not when he's already frightened!"

"Sorry, Miss Jacquie," Samson said mockingly. He twirled the whip in the air an inch above Chance's back, to let her know what he could do if he chose. Jacquetta scrambled down from the wagon. She went to Chance's head and took hold of his bridle. "Easy, boy," she said soothingly. "It's just a bridge. You've crossed bridges before. Give it a try."

Gingerly Chance stepped onto the hollow planks, and Beechnut followed his lead. When they reached the other side Jacquetta climbed back into the wagon. Samson scowled at her, saying nothing.

Jim opened his eyes. "Almost there?" he asked.

"Not yet," Jacquetta said. "How are you doing?"

"Never felt better," he said with a feeble grin.

"It was a silly question, I guess," Jacquetta said. She felt herself blushing.

"You look a lot like my little sister," he said. "Same smile."

He fell silent and closed his eyes again. Peace put her finger to her lips and Jacquetta nodded. They sat quietly for a long time, watching him sleep. The wagon glided across miles of empty countryside. No hands worked the fields. No riders galloped past. Jacquetta felt as though they were moving through a dream. There was only the rocking of the wagon and the soft thud of the horses' hooves on the hard-packed road.

"Stop right here," she told Samson as they came to the bend half a mile from Green Haven. "Better unhitch the horses."

Samson didn't seem to hear her. He rounded the bend and started up the rise.

"We're close enough," Jacquetta called. "Stop right here!"

Samson didn't even turn his head. He was deliberately ignoring her. "Samson, stop!" she shouted. "We can't go this close!"

Samson cracked the whip and the horses broke into a jouncing gallop. They knew where they were, and they were eager to return to their familiar barn.

Wakened by the jolting, Jim moaned and opened his eyes. "Samson!" Jacquetta cried. "Samson, stop!"

It was too late. As they reached the crown of the rise a red-haired Yankee soldier stepped in front of them. Rifle drawn, he ordered the wagon to halt. Samson dragged on the reins and the horses drew to a stop, their flanks heaving and flecked with sweat. With a smug glance in Jacquetta's direction, Samson sprang down from the seat.

"How many of you are there?" the soldier demanded. Jacquetta recognized him; he was Captain Ross.

Samson made a brisk salute. "Four, sir," he said. "Me, the two girls back there, and the wounded Yankee we've brought you."

"Get down," Captain Ross said, gesturing. Jacquetta and Peace clambered to the ground. Captain Ross studied them closely. "Who are you, young lady?" he asked Jacquetta.

It would be useless to give a false name, she decided. If the captain marched her to the big house, the slaves would recognize her. Besides, she could count on Samson to give her away. She drew herself up straight. She'd been taught to be a lady, she reminded herself. It was time to act the part. As sweetly as if she were presenting herself at a ball, she said, "I'm Jacquetta May Logan, sir."

"Your family lives here?" the captain asked in his clipped Yankee speech.

Not any more, she wanted to answer. Not since you set the cotton on fire and drove us out! But she kept her thoughts to herself and said politely, "Why, yes."

Captain Ross blew a blast on a brass whistle that hung around his neck. The door burst open. Captain Harris and two other Yankees hurried out. In moments they set to work, lifting Jim on his mattress and carrying him into the house. When they had gone Captain Ross turned back to Jacquetta. "Beautiful horses you've got there," he said, patting Beechnut's neck. "Fine stock, those Logan Morgans."

Jacquetta's heart seemed to stop. Did the captain suspect that she had something to do with the disappearance of Samoset and the others? The Yankees would never let go of Chance and Beechnut now that they were back at Green Haven.

"Put the horses in the barn," Captain Ross told Samson. "And you, Miss Logan – come with me. Colonel Matthews will want to ask you some questions."

✳ Chapter Nine ✳

Jacquetta hadn't set foot in the big house since she left to visit Cousin Mattie. She felt as though she'd lived through three lifetimes since that morning when she and Papa set out for Brookmoor. She could scarcely believe that less than two weeks had passed.

On the outside the house looked the same, if she pretended away the Yankee sentry. But inside her home was gone, and a Yankee hospital had been set up in its place. Cots stood in the parlour, in the sitting room, and in the music room beside Mama's piano. On every cot lay a man, some asleep, some talking or calling out, some groaning in pain. Here and there blood spattered the floors. The smell of illness and decay hung in the air like a heavy fog.

Colonel Matthews had taken over Papa's study. He sat at Papa's broad mahogany desk, shelves of leather-bound books on three walls around him. Jacquetta stood in the doorway, her knees shaking. For days she had been trying to elude the Yankees. Now she was caught, and about to be questioned by the enemy.

"Come in, Miss Logan," Colonel Matthews said, waving her toward a seat. His mouth smiled, but his eyes were serious, appraising her. "You brought Lieutenant Scarborough from a plantation over near Phantom Swamp, is that correct?"

For a moment she looked at him, baffled. "Oh!" she blurted. "Jim! You mean Jim, sir?"

"Lieutenant James Scarborough, yes. I understand he was attacked by Rebels on the road."

Jacquetta was pretty sure it was the Yankees who did the attacking. Nevertheless, she answered, "Yes, sir."

"Is there much Rebel activity in that area? Have

you seen any troops marching?"

"No, sir, I haven't." She remembered the little band of men in grey uniforms passing the Willard house. They hadn't exactly been marching, and surely they were long gone by now.

The colonel wrote something in a notebook. "Where is your father?" he asked. "Why didn't he ride over with you today?"

"My people left when—" Jacquetta trailed off, confused. She didn't want to say any more than was absolutely necessary. "I was at Deerfield visiting Miss Lucinda Willard," she finished. It wasn't quite true, but it was close enough to be believable.

"I see." Colonel Matthews frowned. "Is it the custom in these parts for grown men to run off and leave little girls by themselves?"

Little girl! How dare he call her that! If he only knew all the grown-up things she'd done over the past few days! But he mustn't find out, that was just the point. He must never learn she had taken the horses that were meant for the Union army.

"No, sir," she said. "It would never happen in ordinary times."

"Where is your father now?" Colonel Matthews pursued.

"I don't know," she said. "I think he and Mama went to Alexandria in Louisiana."

"Yes, that part of Louisiana is still in Rebel hands," the Colonel said. "And what are your plans, Miss Logan, now that you've brought Lieutenant Scarborough to us?"

"I want to go to Alexandria, too," Jacquetta said simply. Her eyes filled with tears and her voice broke as she added, "I don't know how I'm going to get there."

"Well, maybe we can be of help," the colonel said, and the smile found its way to his eyes. "No need to be frightened, young lady. We won't hurt you. We're fighting Rebel soldiers, not women and children."

What about the fields you burn, she wanted to ask him. What about the babies you spear on bayonets? What was the truth and what was wild imagining? "Thank you, sir," she said, returning his smile. "I need to go as soon as I can."

"We'll see what's to be done," Colonel Matthews said, pushing back his chair.

"Meanwhile, you can make yourself useful. Find Doc Graham. Give him a hand with those poor boys out there."

"Yes, sir," Jacquetta said. He had been kind, but he'd never turn her into a Yankee. She wouldn't salute the way Samson did, she told herself fiercely. Instead she rose and made a neat curtsey. Miss Woodworth would have been proud of her.

Jacquetta found Doc Graham in Ward Two, as they now called the sitting room, unwinding a blood-soaked bandage from what was left of a young man's right foot. The doctor was a tall, thin man with stooped shoulders and a weary face. "Colonel Matthews told me to help you," Jacquetta said. "What can I do?"

Doc Graham barely looked up. "Go to the pump and bring a bucket of water," he said. "Then wash that bundle of bedding over there. Boil it first. Then scrub."

Jacquetta had never known that buckets of water were so heavy. She had never guessed that the stains on muslin sheets could be so foul and so difficult to scrub away. She had never imagined that wounded men could groan in such terrible agony. She didn't stop to think that the wounded men and boys were all Yankees. She worked because so much needed to be done, and her hands could be of help.

The heat was constant and inescapable. There wasn't a moment to spare for picking up a fan or slipping out to the shade on the veranda. The work went on and on, each task flowing into the next. Jacquetta washed clothes beside Iza at the washboard, then helped a slave girl called Lindy carry trays of food from the kitchen. Some of the patients were too weak to feed themselves. Jacquetta knelt beside them, spooning stew into their slack mouths, wiping their chins, giving them sips of tepid water. Now and then a man murmured "thank you" before she moved on to the next cot.

Hank was a skinny boy from Pennsylvania, burning up with a fever. Jacquetta was pressing a damp cloth to his forehead when Peace called in a low voice, "Hello, Miss Jacquie!" Apparently Peace had been put to work, too. She bent over a boy two cots down, coaxing him to eat. The boy was Jim.

Jim's wounded arm was propped high on pillows and wrapped in clean bandages. He smiled over at Jacquetta. "Katie?" he said feebly.

"It's Jacquetta. I look like Katie, though."

"Just as pretty," he murmured. "We'll go for a ride... to the river..." He closed his eyes. His head sank back and Peace put down the spoon.

"He wanders in his mind," Peace whispered. "They givin' him powders for the pain. He can't hardly keep awake."

"I wish they all could rest," Jacquetta sighed. "Them, and us too."

"No rest for us," Peace said cheerfully. "I've got to pump some more water. Come help me."

Jacquetta staggered after her to the yard. A light breeze had sprung up, and it was a little cooler outside. She leaned against a tree, her eyes half-closed with exhaustion, as Peace worked the creaky pump handle. "New Orleans is under the Yankees now," Peace said. "I talk to Wit 'bout goin' there to look for Mama. Turn out he been thinkin' 'bout the same thing."

"So you'll both go then?" Jacquetta asked.

"We'll go with you when you start for

Alexandria," Peace said. "We all have to cross the river somehow."

"I'm so tired I can hardly cross the yard," Jacquetta sighed.

Peace cast a furtive glance toward the house. "Chance and Beechnut is in the woods," she whispered. "Samson put 'em in the barn. Wit and me took 'em out."

Jacquetta wished she'd felt relief at the news. All the way to Green Haven she'd worried about how they would keep the horses safe, and now Peace and Wit had managed to rescue them a second time. But suppose Colonel Matthews grew suspicious? Maybe he wouldn't help her get to Alexandria after all. Maybe the whole story would come out, and he would decide to hold her prisoner as a horsethief. "What will the Yankees think, with so many horses disappearing?" she asked fearfully.

Peace gave a mischievous laugh. "Iza say they think Rebels took Samoset and the rest. They thinks it was a sneaky band of Rebels!"

"Does Samson know Chance and Beechnut are gone?"

"He busy tryin' to make Major Landor take notice o' him. Samson ask can he join the Yankee army. The major say he got no unit for coloured boys. Can't give him no rifle. But Samson still tryin'. He say can't they use him as a scout then? Major Landor say they'll see."

The thought of Samson made Jacquetta feel uneasy. To gain points with the Yankees he'd be on the lookout, ready to report anything amiss. It was a miracle that Peace and Wit had managed to hide the horses again. Even if the Yankees were too busy to notice that Chance and Beechnut were gone, no doubt Samson would find out.

Peace seemed to read her thoughts. "We need to get away soon as we can," she said. "'Fore Samson find out them horses missin' again."

Jacquetta knew Peace was right. Yet she was so exhausted she could barely stand upright. To flee tonight was unthinkable. "I can't do it!" she pleaded, covering her face with her hands. "Not now! I can't ride another night with Yankees chasing me – I can't!"

"What you think to do 'stead o' that, Miss Jacquie?" Peace asked.

"I want to wait till morning," Jacquetta said. "Colonel Matthews said maybe he'll help me."

"But by tomorrow Samson mighta found Chance and Beechnut and brought 'em back again," Peace protested.

"I know," Jacquetta said. "It's a chance we've got to take."

When they went back into the house, Jacquetta slipped into the servants' pantry and up the back stairs to the second floor. She wanted to stand in her own bedroom and drink in its comfort. She longed to see all the things she had left behind when she went to Brookmoor – her shelf of books, her chest of drawers, the picture she'd painted at Miss Woodworth's of two dappled colts in a field.

The door to her room stood ajar, and men's voices drifted out into the hall. The Yankees had taken over the upstairs, too. Jacquetta crept back down to the pantry and looked for another place to sleep.

None of the choices were very appealing, but she was too tired to care. She ended up on a heap of dirty blankets someone had tossed in a corner of the kitchen. People came in and out, clattering pans, banging spoons and talking loudly above her. Sometime after midnight she sat up, knowing she wouldn't be able to fall asleep again. She might as well go back to the hospital rooms and see what she could do to help.

A few slaves still hurried to and fro, but the house was quieter now. Some of the wounded men moaned in their sleep. Jacquetta tiptoed over to Jim's cot and looked into his face. He stirred and smiled up at her. "Hello, Jacquetta," he said. "Do you have time to sit with me for a while?"

Jacquetta sat on the floor beside his cot. "I thought you'd be sleeping," she said in a low voice.

He grimaced. "Arm hurts. My leg's not too happy either." After a moment he added, "The doctor's going to cut that ball out of my arm sometime tomorrow."

"Are you scared?" Jacquetta asked.

"Maybe if you talk to me I can think about something else."

"What should I talk about?" Jacquetta asked.

"This is your house, isn't it? What was it like to

grow up here?"

"It was wonderful," Jacquetta said. "We had the whole house to play in, and all the woods and fields, and lots of horses to ride. Mama always wants me to sew and paint china, things young ladies are supposed to like. But Papa says it's not healthy to stay indoors all the time. I think he's right, because I'm almost never sick."

She stopped. For a few moments she missed Papa more than she could bear.

"You have horses," Jim prompted her. "Lots of horses to ride?"

"Morgans," she explained. "We raise them, you know. Or, we used to."

"Until the war?"

"Until the Yankees," Jacquetta said. "They took most of our horses for the army." Again she broke off. Jim was a Yankee himself. How was it possible she was telling him these things about her own life? She didn't feel as though she was talking to an enemy. If it weren't for the uniform and the clipped Yankee way of speaking, how could you tell a Yankee from a Rebel?

Hank, the boy two cots down, moaned and

muttered restlessly. Jacquetta rose and tucked his blanket around him. "Where's the rest of your family?" Jim asked when she settled beside him again.

"They headed to Louisiana. My papa's brother lives there." She drew a deep breath. "I need to go look for them."

"By yourself?" Jim's voice rose sharply. From across the room someone called, "Leave me alone! It ain't time to wake up!"

"You'll never get through," Jim said, whispering again. "They'll stop you. You won't get past the Union lines."

"What do you mean?"

"This part of Mississippi is in Union hands since Vicksburg. No one can cross into Rebel territory, it's not allowed. They'd take you prisoner. They could shoot you as a spy."

"Colonel Matthews said maybe he can help me," Jacquetta said. "I should have left tonight but I'm waiting to find out if he will."

"He's so busy – I hope he remembers." Jim leaned up on his good arm. "Listen," he said. "You probably saved my life, bringing me over here. I'll remind the colonel you're here. I'll ask him to give you a letter."

"What kind of letter?"

"A letter of safe passage."

"What do I do with it?"

"You show it to any Union soldier who questions you," Jim explained. "It says you have permission to cross into Rebel territory to join your family."

"Do you think Colonel Matthews would write me a letter like that?" Jacquetta asked.

"Maybe. I'm assistant to a friend of his, Colonel Titus from the Ninth New Hampshire. Colonel Matthews might do me a special favour. Next time he comes in here I'll ask him."

"Thank you," Jacquetta said with relief. "I don't know how I can thank you enough!"

"I haven't done anything yet," he reminded her. "Wait and see."

✳ Chapter Ten ✳

Hank, the boy with the fever, died just before dawn. From the doorway to the parlour Jacquetta watched Iza and another woman wrap him gently in a clean sheet. When they were done, Captain Ross and two of the men servants carried him out of the house to a spot behind the horse paddock. That patch of meadow had become the burying-ground for Yankee soldiers who breathed their last at the plantation. It was strange to know that forever afterward Green Haven would have a Yankee graveyard.

Jacquetta was bending over the washboard when Samson came quietly up beside her. "Miss

Jacquie, Colonel Matthews want to see you."

Maybe the colonel was calling her in to issue a new set of orders. Or maybe he would tell her that a letter of safe passage was out of the question. But maybe, just maybe, he would offer his help.

Jacquetta's heart leapt with hope as she followed Samson into the house. He led the way to Papa's study. When they saw the colonel Samson saluted and stood at attention just inside the door. Jacquetta remembered what Peace had told her, how Samson was determined to win the trust of the Yankee officers and be made a scout for the Union army. She wished Colonel Matthews would send him out of the room. From where he stood Samson would hear every word that passed between them.

"Good morning, Miss Logan," Colonel Matthews said from behind the mahogany desk. "Do you still wish to leave us?"

"You've all been very kind to me," she said, "but I need to join my family."

"Alexandria, Louisiana is a long way from here. It will be a hard journey."

"Yes, sir, I know."

The colonel opened a drawer in Papa's desk. He drew out a folded sheet of paper and stamped it with a heavy brass seal. He handed the page to Jacquetta.

"To Whom It May Concern," she read, "I, the undersigned, do hereby authorize the bearer of this letter, Miss Jacquetta May Logan of Green Haven Plantation, to travel freely and in safety on the roads and byways of Mississippi. The aforesaid Miss Logan shall hereby be permitted to cross Union lines into territory which still lies in enemy hands, in order that she may be reunited with her family in Louisiana. I humbly request that you treat her with all due courtesy and respect." It was signed "Colonel Augustus Matthews, Thirty-sixth Massachusetts Brigade, United States Army."

"Thank you!" she breathed. "Oh Colonel Matthews, thank you so very, very much!"

In her joy and relief she almost forgot about Samson. Suddenly he spoke behind her. "Colonel Matthews, sir, excuse me for interrupting, but may I give you some information?"

"Is it important, Samson?"

"Yes, sir, I believe it is. You see, I stabled two

horses right and proper yesterday, like Cap'n Ross tell me to. This morning, sir, them horses done disappeared."

The colonel's eyebrows shot up in surprise. "Are you certain, Samson?"

"Quite sure, sir."

Stay calm, Jacquetta commanded herself. Act as though this has nothing to do with you. She tried to put away her precious letter, but her hands shook so much that she couldn't find her apron pocket. Samson had found a way to prove himself. He was being a vigilant scout for the Yankees.

Colonel Matthews looked straight past her. "Do you have any idea where these horses may be?" he asked Samson.

Samson stepped farther into the room. He stood beneath the sunlit window, where Jacquetta could see his triumphant grin. "Yes, sir, I do. They're safe in the barn again, sir. I found them and brought them back."

"Very good," Colonel Matthews said warmly. "Do you have any idea how the horses left the barn in the first place?"

"No sir," Samson said. He added slyly, "But

maybe Miss Jacquie got some notion."

Colonel Matthews turned in his chair to face her. Again she saw a friendly smile on his lips, a smile that didn't reach his eyes. "All right, Miss Logan," he said quietly, "what can you tell me about the horses you brought from the Willard plantation?"

Speak calmly, she repeated to herself. Speak strongly and clearly, as if you're in elocution class. "They're not Willard horses, sir," she explained. "They're from our Green Haven stables. One is a roan mare called Beechnut. The other one is my own bay gelding, Chance."

"And how did they vanish from the barn?"

"I was afraid the Yankees – the Union soldiers – would take them and..." Her voice shook dangerously, "use them in the army. I hid them in the woods to save them."

She hadn't hidden Chance and Beechnut – not this time, anyway. Peace and Wit had taken them. She herself wasn't responsible. Why had she chosen to lie and put herself in jeopardy? Maybe the colonel would take back his letter now. Maybe he'd put her on trial as a common horse thief.

But she couldn't tell the colonel what had really happened. Peace and Wit were slaves. If they were caught, even by the Yankees, anything might happen to them. A slave had no rights. It had been that way for as long as anyone could remember. People said the Yankees were fighting to free the slaves, but how would they treat one who made off with their horses? In the Delta slaves were beaten, starved, locked up, even hanged, for far smaller offences, and no law protected them. Jacquetta couldn't tell Colonel Matthews what Wit and Peace had done. She had no choice but to take the blame upon herself.

"You made off with two horses alone?" Colonel Matthews demanded.

"Yes, sir." She glanced sideways at Samson, wondering if he would give her away. For the first time she saw a glimmer of respect, even warmth in his face. His head moved almost imperceptibly in a small, secret nod of approval.

"How old are you, Miss Logan?" Colonel Matthews asked.

"I'm fourteen. I'll be fifteen in January."

The colonel tilted back in his chair. For a few

moments he gazed at the ceiling. "They raise spunky young ladies in these parts, don't they?" he exclaimed. Then suddenly, amazingly, he laughed. "I imagine you would like to take those two fine Morgans with you across the Union lines. Am I right, Miss Logan?"

Jacquetta nodded mutely. Any wrong word might destroy his good humour.

"The Union army needs horses very badly," he went on. "We commandeered twenty-three excellent specimens the day we arrived. A band of Rebels made off with half a dozen more." He hesitated and looked at her questioningly. She gazed back, fighting to keep her eyes steady, to reveal nothing. "And now we have two in the stable. Two more strong, healthy Morgans to serve our country. Why should I let you take them away to Rebel territory? Tell me that!"

Jacquetta began slowly, choosing her words with care. "You've taken our house," she said. "You need a hospital for the soldiers, and our house is just right. So in a way – it's hard to explain – I don't mind about that any more. And you're using other things, too – the flour and cornmeal and molasses we stored, the vegetables from our garden and the eggs from our henhouse. Twenty-three of our horses — you've taken them." Her voice trembled. She tried to steady herself with a deep breath, but it didn't help. "Chance is all that's left!" she cried. "I raised him from a colt! I trained him myself! He comes when I whistle! Please, please let me keep him!"

"Persuasive, too," the colonel said, half to himself. "Persuasive and passionate, and spunky besides."

Once Jacquetta had seen a cat playing with a mouse on a hot summer afternoon. The cat had been almost too sleepy to move. It had held the mouse lightly, indifferently, under one paw, pondering its fate. Jacquetta felt like that mouse now. Her fate and the fate of Chance rested in the colonel's hands.

"It was a heavy loss for us when the Rebs ran off with that bunch of horses the other night," he said at last. Again he paused, waiting for some response from her. Again Jacquetta said nothing. "I can't allow you to take these last two with you."

Jacquetta's heart gave a terrible lurch. She

couldn't breathe. Tears stung her eyes. She wouldn't let him see her cry, she thought. Whatever happened, she would never cry in front of this smug Yankee officer.

"Still," the colonel went on, "we can spare one. We'll keep the mare. Take the gelding. He's yours."

All her brave resolve did no good at all. Jacquetta burst into tears. "Thank you, sir! How can I thank you enough?"

"I wish I could send an escort with you," Colonel Matthews said. "But I need every man I've got just now."

"I'll be all right, sir. I'm used to travelling."

"What do you call that horse of yours? Chance?" Once more a true smile sparkled from his eyes. "You're taking a real risk out on those roads, letter or no letter. I hope your Chance will bring you luck."

"Goodbye, ol' lady," Peace murmured, patting Beechnut's neck. She held out a generous lump of sugar, a parting present. Beechnut took it and nuzzled Peace's shoulder. Jacquetta saw Peace give her a final hug before she shut the stall door softly behind her.

Maybe Peace loved Beechnut almost as much as she loved Chance. Jacquetta hadn't thought twice about sacrificing Beechnut to save Chance from the Yankees. She'd never considered Peace's feelings, or what Peace would have done if the choice were hers. "Maybe they'll keep Beechnut here," Jacquetta said awkwardly. "They could use her to fetch supplies for the hospital."

"Maybe," Peace said tersely. "It gonna be full dark soon. We better go."

Jacquetta checked Chance's saddlebags. They were well-packed with food for the journey. There was only one more thing she had to do. "I'll be right back," she told Peace. "I want to say goodbye to Jim."

The first thing Jacquetta noticed when she entered the parlour was the empty cot where Hank had lain. She averted her gaze and hurried past it to Jim's cot. Jim was asleep. She watched him for a moment, not wanting to wake him. Then she tiptoed to Mama's table in the corner. There was still ink in the inkstand, and paper in the drawer.

"Dear Jim," she wrote. "Thank you for all your help. Colonel Matthews has given me a letter of safe passage, and I'm off to find my mother and father. I hope you get home safely and have many more rides with your sister Katie. I hope this war will be over soon! I will always remember you." She pondered the closing and finally wrote, "With love, Jacquetta May Logan."

"Goodbye," she whispered, slipping the note beneath his pillow. He didn't open his eyes. Only the rise and fall of his light blanket told her that he was still alive.

Peace and Wit had Chance out in the yard by the time Jacquetta returned. "He can carry both you girls," Wit said. "I'll follow along. We goin' to Deerfield first."

From the Willard place it wasn't far to the hidden clearing in the swamp. No one said it aloud, but Jacquetta guessed they were all thinking about the rest of the horses. Could they possibly get them all to Louisiana? Would they be risking too much if they tried?

✳ Chapter Eleven ✳

If she had learned anything through these extraordinary adventures, Jacquetta mused, it was how to travel at night. They set out from Green Haven as twilight descended and the summer heat began to release its grip on the day. The night sounds of owls and insects seemed friendly now, and the dim shapes of trees meant safety. Danger lay in daylight and the open road.

They reached Deerfield after a ride of nearly three hours. As soon as she saw them, Miss Rachel bustled about, bringing them fried chicken and peach cobbler.

The house was quiet tonight. There was no sign of the party of two nights ago. "A lot of our people settin' out to look for their kinfolks," Miss Rachel explained. "Gonna be meetin's of the long lost all over the country pretty soon."

They all seemed to assume that the Willards were never coming back, Jacquetta thought. Where the Yankees were in control, slavery was no more. But the war wasn't over, and the Rebels weren't beaten yet. What would become of Miss Rachel and Peace and the others if the Rebels managed to win in the end? Would they all have to live as slaves again?

"How far's New Orleans?" Peace asked.

"It's a long way," Miss Rachel sighed, shaking her head. "Way down the river."

"That's where they sent our mama," Peace said. "That's where Wit and me are goin'."

Miss Rachel frowned and clicked her tongue, but she didn't argue. Peace had made up her mind.

"How can we get across the river?" Jacquetta asked. "Can we get a ferry?"

Miss Rachel pondered. "Last summer I went with Miss Lucinda out to Natchitoches. Was a ferry at Beaufort's Landing."

"Does it still run, do you think?" Jacquetta asked.

Miss Rachel shrugged. "Could be," she said. "Rebels still holdin' the river above Baton Rouge. You got a good chance o' findin' somethin'."

"Beaufort's Landing," Jacquetta mused. "How big a place is it?"

"They got a store with a post office," Miss Rachel said. "It's big enough for that."

A store, Jacquetta thought with a lurch somewhere in her chest. A store might have a newspaper with some news of the men killed at Vicksburg. Maybe she would be able to find out if Marcus and Adam were still alive.

Suddenly Wit spoke up. "How we gonna take all them horses over on a ferry?" he demanded. "How we even gonna get 'em to the river without the Yankees stoppin' us? Better we take three for ridin' and leave the rest here."

Jacquetta saw his point. They could travel faster if they weren't leading a string of riderless horses. But she hated to think of abandoning any more of the horses now that they'd come this far. When they found a ferry — *if* they found one — they'd figure out how to get the horses across.

"We already left Beechnut!" Peace burst out.

"We ain't leavin' no more o' them. If we can ride three we can bring the others along!"

"Miss Rachel make sure they safe right here," Wit insisted.

Peace stood her ground. "What Miss Rachel gonna do when the Yankees come? Or the Rebels? Either one gonna take whatever horses they find and put 'em in the fightin'!"

"They'll take them from us, too, if they stop us," Wit pointed out.

"Wait," Jacquetta told them. "I have a letter from Colonel Matthews. It says the Yankees should treat me with courtesy. I think we'll be all right." She drew the envelope from her pocket and held it out for everyone to see.

The idea of the letter seemed to carry weight. It was as though the colonel's promise on the printed page held some sort of magic for them all. Even Wit finally agreed that they should get the horses from the swamp and take them all to safety in Louisiana.

The grandfather clock was striking midnight when they left the house. Wit led the way into the swamp. He glided among the moss-cloaked trees, leading them from one bit of solid ground to another on an invisible path he seemed to know by heart. Suddenly Chance lifted his head and gave a neigh of greeting. From the distance came Samoset's proud, clear reply.

"They're all here!" Jacquetta cried joyfully when they reached the clearing. The horses' manes and tails were matted with burrs, mud caked their legs and bellies, but they looked healthy and alert. Full of curiosity, they crowded toward the little party of humans.

Jacquetta, Peace and Wit worked quickly, fastening bridles and attaching leads. Slapping at the relentless mosquitoes that hummed around their faces, they checked all of the horses' hooves for stones. At last they were on the move. Wit headed the procession on Samoset, leading Dorcas. Now that Beechnut was gone Peace rode Cass, the sweetest-tempered mare in the group, with Jilly on a lead rope. Jacquetta, on Chance, led Tina.

They made slow progress at first, working their way westward through the swamp. When they emerged into the open woods they picked up their pace. Jacquetta patted her apron pocket and felt the reassuring folds of Colonel Matthews' letter. Safe passage! The words sang in her head like a Sunday hymn. They had Colonel Matthews' protection.

Of course Colonel Matthews didn't know that *they* were the Rebels who had made off with the horses from the barn. It didn't feel quite right to deceive him this way. He had tried to be kind to her. He could have kept Chance and sent her off on foot. But they weren't stealing, she reminded herself. They were rescuing Green Haven property. If she could help it, no more Green Haven Morgans would ever go to war.

Letter or no letter, it was best to stay out of sight. They kept to the woods until almost daybreak. Wit knew a place where they could rest during the daylight hours, but it lay on the far side of a wide dirt road. Jacquetta waited with the horses while Wit scouted off to the right and Peace to the left. In a few minutes they were back. "All clear," Peace said. "Let's go."

They clattered across the road three abreast, the horses jingling their bridles with pleasure at being out in the open again. Chance kicked up his heels and whinnied with delight. From somewhere in the woods ahead came a shout. Before Jacquetta could think what to do, a blue-uniformed soldier stepped out of the trees, a rifle resting on his shoulder. "Halt!" he ordered. "Stop right where you are!"

Jacquetta drew Chance to a stop. Beside her Peace and Wit reined in their mounts. The horses stamped and quivered, eager to follow the road.

The Yankee didn't bother with niceties. He pointed the rifle at Jacquetta and demanded, "Where you going?"

It was hard to keep her voice steady as she looked into the barrel of the gun. "We're on the way to Beaufort's Landing," she said, smiling as sweetly as she could manage. "We're about to take the ferry."

"You've got to cross Union lines to do that," the soldier said. "Rebels ain't allowed."

"I know that," said Jacquetta. "I have permission from Colonel Matthews."

"Who's he?"

Jacquetta's heart sank. She'd thought every Yankee in Mississippi knew Colonel Matthews' name.

"Colonel Augustus Mathews," she said. "Of the Thirty-sixth Massachusetts." She drew out the letter and unfolded it gingerly.

"Let me see that!" the soldier exclaimed. He reached up and snatched the paper from her hand. For a few moments he studied it intently. At last he grunted and handed it back to her. With a jolt of surprise, Jacquetta saw that he had been holding the page upside down. He hadn't read a word. He didn't know how to read at all.

He turned his attention to the horses. "What you doing with those nags?"

Nags! Jacquetta wanted to flare in indignation. *You don't know horses, do you?*

Her gaze travelled over the Morgans. They really didn't look like much, mud-caked and bedraggled as they were. Maybe it was just as well. "Oh," she said, almost apologetically, "they're some old workhorses from a plantation upriver." She groped through her memory, hunting for a name she had heard somewhere – yes, Jim had mentioned someone... "Colonel Matthews asked me to take them to his friend, Colonel Titus."

The soldier frowned. "My feet sure are sore," he

said. "I could use one of them nags to take me where I'm going."

"Colonel Titus needs every horse he can get," Jacquetta said. "We're to deliver them all to him directly."

"Your colonel can spare one nag for a fellow American. Tell him my horse took a bullet at Vicksburg." He pointed at Samoset. "That big boy there would suit me fine."

"You can't—" Jacquetta began.

Suddenly Wit uttered a wild yell and dug his heels into the stallion's flanks. Samoset leapt forward and thundered into the woods. The Yankee raised his gun to his shoulder. A shot rang out. Chance lunged in panic and bolted down the road. Over her shoulder Jacquetta saw Cass tear off in the opposite direction, Peace clinging desperately to her back. Jacquetta clutched Chance's reins in one hand and Tina's lead rope in the other. From somewhere behind her came more shots, and she was determined to put as much distance as she could between the Yankee and herself. "Giddap, Chance!" she cried, and he put on an added burst of speed.

When she finally reined Chance to a stop, the woods were awakening around her. The birds were in full chorus, unperturbed by the human commotion. Jacquetta slipped off Chance's back and led the horses off the road. When they were deep among the trees she rubbed them down with handfuls of grass. The familiar circular motion helped to calm her.

The soldier was well behind her, at least for now. But how would she find Peace and Wit again? They had all scattered in different directions. The Yankee would have a hard time tracking them down, but by the same token it would be no easy matter for them to find each other. If she headed back in the direction she had come, she might run into the Yankee — and this time she'd be all alone. For now, she decided, it was best for her to stay where she was. Wit knew the woods better than she or Peace did. He would find them and bring them together when the time was right.

From where they stood she and the horses couldn't be seen from the road. Chance and Tina were already cropping the grass. They seemed content after their wild dash, their fright already forgotten.

Jacquetta leaned against a tree trunk. She remembered the day she watched from a limb of the apple tree and saw the Yankee sentry at Green Haven. She was on sentry duty now, she thought. She had to watch and listen and somehow protect herself and the horses.

It wasn't easy to concentrate on her surroundings. The leafy ceiling created a pleasant shade. Jacquetta slid down to sit in a nest of dead leaves among the tree roots. Her eyelids grew heavy. She jumped up and danced from foot to foot, fighting to stay awake. Chance lifted his head and watched her, puzzled. "I bet you think I've gone crazy," she told him. "I wonder what you'll think of the ferry? It'll rock from side to side, but don't worry. We'll cross the river and everything will be all right."

Chance cocked his ears, taking in the tone of her voice. "I wonder where we'll live in Louisiana," she went on. "Will Uncle James have room for us all?" It was a comfort to say her thoughts aloud. Chance was a perfect audience.

He never interrupted or criticized, but watched her intently with his trusting brown eyes.

Behind her a twig snapped. Jacquetta whirled, her heart racing. No one was there. Maybe it was just a squirrel. Still, she bent down and picked up a large stone. It wouldn't be much help against the Yankee's gun, but she'd fight to her last breath.

Silently a figure separated itself from the shadows. "Miss Jacquie?" said Wit. "Don't be scared. It's me."

"Wit!" she breathed, flooded with relief. "You're all right! I'm so glad to see you! Where's Peace? Where are the horses?"

Wit pointed over his shoulder. "I found Peace. She didn't go far. Come on."

"What about the Yankee?" Jacquetta asked as Wit led the way along a winding deer track.

"He wanderin' off lost," Wit said, chuckling. "I seen him cross the road like he makin' for the swamp."

"He could have killed you," Jacquetta exclaimed. "You risked your life!"

Wit shrugged. "If I let him take Samoset, my

sister'd kill me for sure," he said. "Better take my chances with the Yankee."

After ten minutes the ground dipped to form a grassy hollow. Samoset, Dorcas, Jilly and Cass grazed happily. Peace hurried to greet them. They would stay here for the rest of the day, taking turns to keep watch.

Toward sundown they saddled up again and once more headed west. Jacquetta wasn't sure when they crossed into Confederate territory. To her relief they didn't meet any more soldiers, either Yankees or Rebels.

Within a few miles they saw the reedy bank of the river. Sluggish and brown, the great Mississippi flowed before them. Keeping to the woods they followed it downstream. The distant barking of dogs announced that they were approaching Beaufort's Landing. They stopped in the woods beyond the edge of town and waited for the morning.

Now that they were on Rebel soil, Jacquetta realized, Peace and Wit could no longer travel safely. Any slave walking alone could be seized as a runaway. Unless they were in her company it was best that they not be seen. After some discussion, it was decided that Peace and Wit would stay with Samoset and the mares, while Jacquetta rode Chance into town to ask about the ferry.

Soon after daybreak Jacquetta splashed Chance's legs with water from the river to wash off the mud. Peace helped her loosen some of the burrs from his mane and tail until he looked almost respectable. Jacquetta wished she could say the same for herself. The frock she had borrowed from Lucinda Willard was muddy and torn beyond hope. Anyone would know at a glance that she'd been sleeping under the stars. "Being a lady is all in your carriage," Miss Woodworth used to say. Back straight and head held high, Jacquetta rode into town.

Beaufort's Landing was a collection of shabby little houses strung along a dusty street. At one end of the street stood the building that served as general store and post office. At the other end a steep slope led down to the ferry landing. Two soldiers in grey uniforms marched toward Jacquetta up the street. They looked tired and worn, but they carried their rifles proudly. A boy of twelve or thirteen beat time briskly on a battered drum. Jacquetta smiled at them and raised her hand in a smart salute.

In front of the store she dismounted and tied Chance to the hitching post. A man with a shiny bald head was sweeping the doorstep. "Are you open?" Jacquetta asked.

"Yes'm," he said, waving her inside. The shelves were nearly bare. The only merchandise seemed to be a half-filled keg of nails, some sacks of flour and cornmeal, and a few packets of pins and needles. But on the counter Jacquetta saw what she was looking for, a stack of folded newspapers. The papers were dated July 6, five days ago. Jacquetta took one from the top of the stack and spread it open. There was no lead story. On black-bordered pages she saw column after column of names, hundreds of them − thousands − the list of the dead from the Battle of Vicksburg.

The names were listed alphabetically. With shaking hands Jacquetta turned the pages until she saw Lampert, Langston and Lawrence. Her eyes travelled down the grim column, past Lee, Linton,

Lockley and Lodge. Suddenly there it was: Logan, Pvt Marcus Aurelius. Forty-third Mississippi Brigade."

✳ Chapter Twelve ✳

Of course it was a mistake, she told herself desperately. There were Logans all over Mississippi. It must be some cousin twice removed...

Caught in a nightmare, she read down the list again. Adam's name wasn't there – but there was Marcus's, clear and bold. In the Forty-third Mississippi there could be only one Private Marcus Aurelius Logan.

"You all right, miss?" the storekeeper called after her as she stumbled out to the street. She couldn't speak. She waved him away and mounted Chance again. Out of town, across fields, down a rutted dirt road – she didn't notice where they were going.

Marcus. Marcus. His name echoed and re-echoed in her head. A hundred images of him played behind her eyes: Marcus at the dinner table, talking politics with Papa; Marcus wrestling on the grass with one of the Clarence boys; Marcus in the yard kissing Janie Amberson. How she wished she'd never thrown that apple at him! She hadn't even cried when she said goodbye to him, the time he took her to Miss Woodworth's on the train. If she had only known, that last afternoon in Miss Woodworth's parlour, that she would never see him again! She would have wrapped her arms around him and never let him go.

Chance chose the way back to the others in the woods. Jacquetta had no memory of turning him right or left, but after a while she saw that they had reached the clearing again. She slid to the ground and leaned against Chance's flank. Through a fog she heard Peace's anxious questions, "Miss Jacquie, what's wrong? What is it?"

"It's my brother," she said at last. "My brother Marcus. Killed at Vicksburg."

"Oh, Miss Jacquie! I'm so sorry!" Peace came and stood beside her. She held Jacquetta in her arms as she cried.

Sometime later Jacquetta noticed that the sun was high in the sky. She and Peace were sitting on the grass. Peace was offering her some food from Chance's saddlebag, but Jacquetta couldn't think about eating. She couldn't think about anything.

Gently Peace called her back to the world. "Miss Jacquie," she asked, "you find out when the ferry run?"

"No!" Jacquetta cried. "It doesn't matter any more! Marcus is dead!"

"You got to find your mama and papa," Peace reminded her. "It be a comfort to your people to have you back."

Jacquetta thought of Papa and Mama. She thought of Adam, wherever he was. Did they know about Marcus yet? How would they bear it, any of them? Marcus had always been so level-headed and solid. He couldn't be gone. It wasn't possible!

"Wit can stay with the horses," Peace decided. "I'll go with you to the landing, Miss Jacquie. We'll ask if the ferry go today."

Jacquetta was too numb to resist. They led the horses to the edge of the woods and left Wit in charge. Jacquetta and Peace went into town on foot, as though they were an ordinary mistress and slave. They descended the slope at the end of the street and gazed up and down the river. It flowed past them, muddy and slow. Not a boat was in sight.

For a while they sat on a log and waited. The air was heavy and still. A pair of mallards paddled along the bank. Peace got up and peered into the ferryman's hut. "Look like nobody been here in a long time," she reported.

It was useless to wait any more. They trudged back along the street. The storekeeper leaned in his doorway, a wide-brimmed hat shielding his bald head from the sun. "Where's that pretty bay horse of yours, ma'am?" he asked.

Jacquetta gestured vaguely behind her. "Will the ferry be leaving this afternoon?" she asked.

The storekeeper laughed ruefully. "She hasn't run since May," he said. "The army took her."

"Commandeered." Jacquetta turned away. She

started back down the street. She didn't know where she was going. She didn't care.

Peace caught up with her, and they stood against a rail fence. "There's got to be some way across," Peace said. "We'll find out."

"You heard what he said. We're two months too late."

"Oh, Miss Jacquie! You talk like you givin' it up!"

"I'm done," Jacquetta said simply. "There's nowhere to go from here."

"Don't give up hope," Peace told her. "You keep hope alive, you be all right in the end."

From somewhere in the distance came the clatter of hooves and the rumble of wagon wheels.

At first Jacquetta didn't even turn to look. Blank with despair, she stared down at her feet in the tattered remains of her shoes. The horses drew closer, bearing down on her. Peace grabbed her arm and pulled her out of the way. "Whoa there!" the driver shouted. "Whoa!"

It was an ordinary farm cart, the kind used for carrying fruit and vegetables to market. The only unusual feature was the team, panting and blowing in the traces. They were a pair of coal-black geldings, perfectly matched. She'd only seen a team like that once before, Uncle Silas' prized pair, Jeff and Davis. The grey-haired man holding the reins was strangely familiar, too. She could almost picture him expanding with pride in his chair at the head of the dinner table.

"Uncle Silas?" she asked in amazement. "Is it really you?"

Now she saw two figures huddled in the cart. Aunt Clem peered down, wide-eyed with astonishment. Cousin Mattie cried, "Jacquetta!" and burst into tears.

In the next moment Jacquetta was crying too, sobbing with grief and joy in Aunt Clem's arms. "Thank God you're safe!" Aunt Clem cried. "I didn't know how I'd ever face your mother!"

"We searched the woods all night," Uncle Silas said. "How on earth did you get away so fast?"

"Where have you been all this time?" Mattie asked. "I thought for sure you were dead!"

Jacquetta wished she could answer their questions, but the column of names got in the way of everything else. "I read the newspaper today," she told them. "Have you heard about Marcus?"

"We know," Aunt Clem murmured. "We saw the list the other day."

For a few minutes they were all quiet together. At last Uncle Silas said, "We won't let you disappear again, young lady. We're taking you with us. Before I sign up with the Mississippi Volunteers, I'm taking you all to Clem's brother in Alexandria."

"That's where Mama and Papa went, too," Jacquetta said. "But the ferry doesn't run any more."

"Don't you worry about that," Uncle Silas assured her. "There's a ferryman on his way right now. I met him upriver yesterday. He's one of our boys. A good Rebel. Runs a boat back and forth to help people get away from the Yankees."

"Can he take the horses?" Jacquetta asked, glancing at the team. She added, "There are six more. We brought them from Green Haven."

"How in the world?" Aunt Clem exclaimed.

"Peace helped me," Jacquetta said, "and her brother Wit." She realized suddenly that Peace had edged away and was watching from a distance. She would have liked to call her back, to let Peace help her describe their adventures. But she sensed Peace's uneasiness, and knew that she wanted to stand apart.

In ragged bits and chunks she told the story alone. When she reached the part about helping in the Yankee hospital Aunt Clem was horrified. "You were there all that time, among those Yankees?" she cried. "They could have murdered you!"

"No one tried to hurt me," Jacquetta said. "They helped me. Jim, and Colonel Matthews – they were kind."

Aunt Clem and Mattie shook their heads in disbelief. Uncle Silas brushed her words aside, turning to practical matters. "We can take the horses," he said. "This ferryman, he's got a big flatboat. Plenty of room. There's a sandbar a mile downriver – we'll pole 'er across."

Behind them a door opened. An old woman stepped out and introduced herself as Miss Sarah Summerdale. She invited them all inside for a glass of spring water and something to eat. Jacquetta hadn't realized how thirsty she was. The thought of water was glorious.

As they started up the wooden steps, Jacquetta gestured for Peace to come with them. Peace hesitated. "Come on!" Jacquetta called. "You must be thirsty, too." Peace nodded and followed her inside.

The house was spotless, and Jacquetta felt suddenly ashamed in her filthy frock. Miss Sarah brought a pitcher of water and some salt pork and cheese, apologizing profusely that she didn't have more to offer. "I might just have a spare frock upstairs," she told Jacquetta after they had eaten. "You can have it if it suits you. That way your mama can see you looking fresh and sweet."

Jacquetta and Peace followed Miss Sarah upstairs. Miss Sarah laid a clean frock across the bed and returned to the others below, leaving the two girls alone. Jacquetta was relieved to shed Lucinda Willard's mud-caked frock and petticoats. She slipped gratefully into the clean clothes. They gave her the feeling that she was making a fresh start. In barely an hour she had risen from despair to a renewed sense of hope. Uncle Silas would take her to Mama and Papa. The war had robbed them of their home and their land, and now Marcus, too, was gone. But somehow they would rebuild their lives. She remembered what Peace had told her when she was ready to give up: "You keep hope alive, you be all right in the end."

As she was about to go back downstairs, Peace put out a restraining hand. "Miss Jacquie," she said, "I has to say goodbye to you."

"Goodbye?" Jacquetta repeated, stunned. "What do you mean?"

"You safe now, and the horses safe, too," Peace said. "But me and Wit – we ain't safe here on Rebel land. If they takes us back into slavery, we ain't never gonna find our mama."

"But," Jacquetta began, "nobody's going to—"

"Your uncle maybe," Peace said. "Or that flatboat man. Anyone that sees us! We has to go our own way now."

"Oh, Peace!" Jacquetta cried. "I'm going to miss you so much! I can't say goodbye yet!"

"Soon's we go back down, you distract the others," Peace said. "I gonna slip out the side door and run back to the woods. When you go for the horses, me and Wit'll be gone."

Jacquetta thought of all the things Peace had

done for her since that morning in the barn at Green Haven. Now it was her turn to help Peace. She drew a deep breath. "All right," she said. "I'll say goodbye now. I won't get another chance." She threw her arms around Peace and gave her a long hug. Then they walked sedately downstairs, mistress and servant.

Aunt Clem and Miss Sarah said the frock fit Jacquetta perfectly. Mattie sighed that it was a shame Jacquetta had no clothes left of her own. She said she and Aunt Clem had packed a small trunk before they left Brookmoor. It was on the cart. There would be all sorts of things Jacquetta could wear. Jacquetta was careful to keep them talking. She saw Uncle Silas step out to the street to look for the ferryman. She didn't say a word when she glanced at the place where Peace had been standing, and discovered she was gone.

After a while they all trooped back outside. The ferryman still hadn't arrived, but Uncle Silas was certain he'd be there soon. In the meantime, he suggested, Jacquetta could lead the way to the horses hidden in the woods.

The horses were in the clearing where Jacquetta had last seen them. There was no sign of Wit or Peace. Uncle Silas took charge, fastening lead ropes and her…ding the horses into Beaufort's Landing. They filled the street with their stamping, snorting and neighing. The whole town came out to see them. Children patted them and helped to untangle their manes and tails. The horses seemed to love the attention.

"I still can't quite believe you managed to bring them from Green Haven by yourself!" Aunt Clem told Jacquetta. "I don't know how you survived all alone!"

"I wasn't alone," Jacquetta insisted. "I couldn't have done it without Peace and Wit, and Miss Rachel, and Colonel Matthews, and Jim…"

"Well, apart from servants and Yankees," Aunt Clem said with a wave of her hand, "you had no one to turn to."

"I had help all the way," Jacquetta said firmly, "from a lot of fine people."

"Speaking of servants," Aunt Clem said. "That girl you had with you – Peace. Where is she?"

"She's gone," Jacquetta said. "We won't see her

again."

"She can't just run off!" Aunt Clem exclaimed. "Silas can go after her."

"Don't send him," Jacquetta pleaded. "Let her go. Please."

Aunt Clem was about to protest when Uncle Silas shouted, "Ferry's here! All aboard!"

Everyone crowded down to the landing to see the flatboat, which, amazingly, hadn't yet been commandeered by either the Yankees or the Rebels. The ferryman didn't try to explain how he managed to keep the boat for himself. He grinned a sly, secret grin and took the money Uncle Silas pressed into his palm.

Chance had wandered up the street and was peering curiously into the general store. The storekeeper pointed and chuckled. "Maybe he'd like some nails," he said. "Or a paper of pins."

"Come here, Chance!" Jacquetta called. She gave their special whistle, low-high, like a question. Chance wheeled around and trotted to meet her. She picked up the reins and led him down to the waiting boat.

* * *

*To whet your appetite for another thrilling
adventure in the* Saddle the Wind *series,
read on for the opening chapter of*
Blackwater Creek.

⋆ SADDLE THE WIND ⋆

BLACKWATER CREEK

DEBORAH KENT

CALIFORNIA, 1849
AND THE GOLD RUSH IS ON...

Erika Nagy and her family have come to California from Hungary in search of gold. When their gold pans remain empty and they cannot pay the rent, Erika must go to work for their mean landlord, the rancher Hart Latham. At the ranch Erika forms a special bond with an injured filly, named Arany, that she nurses back to health. When Arany escapes from the corral, Erika searches for her at Blackwater Creek – and finds much more than she bargained for!

✳ Chapter One ✳

Gripping handholds among the rocks, Erika scrambled to the crest of the ravine. She paused to catch her breath and looked carefully around her. Her ears strained for a telltale crackle in the underbrush, but she heard only the sigh of the wind. "Virag!" she called. "Come on, Virag! It's milking time!"

Where had that empty-headed cow wandered now? This was the third time she'd broken out of the pasture. A week ago old Hart Latham had caught her grazing calmly at the edge of his hayfield. "If I catch that bohunk cow of yours in my fields again I'll shoot her!" Latham had warned when Erika went to fetch her.

Papa told Erika and her brother Sandor to keep Virag off Latham's land, and not to set foot there themselves. Virag, however, had her own ideas on the subject. She seemed convinced that the wild flowers in Hart Latham's fields were tastier than anything the Nagys' pasture could offer her.

But Virag wasn't in the hayfield this time. She must have strayed even farther. Erika didn't doubt Hart Latham would shoot her on sight – if a cougar didn't get her first. Erika shoved those thoughts deep into a back corner of her mind. The Nagys couldn't afford the loss of their only cow, not even a troublemaker like Virag.

Pebbles rolled beneath her feet as Erika made her way along the ridge. Soon the ground sloped down to a grassy hollow, just the sort of place Virag preferred. Virag would go to any lengths to find flowers to munch on. Her tastes had earned her the name *Virag* – "flower" in Hungarian. Searching and calling, Erika waded through waist-high grass that rippled around her like water. Hidden grasshoppers rasped out their springtime music. A quail started up at her feet and hurtled away with a cry of alarm. But there was no sign of the spotted cow.

Sighing, Erika started up the next rise and when she reached the top, she gasped in dismay.

Before her stood Hart Latham's stable, a low-slung log building with a red-tiled roof. Beyond the stable loomed the ranch house itself. She hadn't realised that her search had brought her so deep into Latham's territory. She wondered who would be more furious – Latham or her father – if he knew she was here. She should get away before anyone caught her! But Erika couldn't tear herself away from what she saw.

Four horses stood in the corral adjoining the stable. Three of them grazed quietly. The fourth, a little sorrel filly, craned her neck over the top of the fence. Erika couldn't resist. She had to get a closer look.

Ever since her family started renting a parcel of Latham's land four months ago, Erika had seen horses come and go from his fields. Horse-trading was one of Latham's businesses, in addition to raising cattle and working gold claims on the Stanislaus River. He and his ranch hands bought horses from other traders, or caught them in the mountains and broke them to the saddle. With so many people flooding into the hills to look for gold, horses were always in demand.

Each time she saw one, Erika had longed to feed Latham's horses and curry them. She had yearned to ride them along California's stony mountain trails. Back in Hungary, Erika's grandmother used to tend all the horses in their village. She liked to take Erika along when she went to treat a horse with colic or a mare in foal. "Watch and learn, my *lanyaunoka*," her grandmother would say. "Some day you'll be taking care of these horses, instead of me."

"Yes, *Naganya,*" Erika would say, feeling proud that her grandmother had such faith in her. But Erika's contact with horses had ended abruptly when she and her family left Hungary two years ago, back in 1847. Until today, she had only looked from a distance, silent and wishful.

Erika approached the corral slowly. The horses looked like mustangs, wiry and sure-footed, the sort that ran wild in the mountains. A pinto and two palominos bunched in the farthest corner, but the sorrel stayed at the fence. Erika stretched out her hand, and the filly touched it with her velvet nose. Her golden coat glistened, in lovely contrast to her black mane and tail. A name sprang into Erika's mind, the perfect name for this beautiful filly. "Arany!" she said. *Arany* was the Hungarian word for gold.

The pinto and the palominos twitched their ears and watched cautiously. Then, the pinto gave a short whinny, and Arany left Erika to join the other horses. As the filly crossed the paddock, Erika saw that she favoured her right foreleg. Something was wrong. Erika had to find out what.

Latham's fence was almost as flimsy as the fence to Virag's pasture. The gate sagged on its hinges. Erika unlatched it carefully and entered the corral. "*Szegenyem!*" she murmured in Hungarian. "You poor thing! What's the matter? Let me see."

The filly sidled away for a moment, then stood still and let Erika examine her leg. Erika ran her hands over the cannon and pastern to the hoof, as

Naganya had taught her back in the old country. The front of the foreleg felt warm and swollen along the cannon bone, and the filly flinched away at Erika's touch.

Shinsore, Erika thought. Maybe someone had ridden her too hard, or perhaps she'd been doing some hard running on her own. The cause didn't matter now. But if Arany's problem went untreated, the filly might become permanently lame. No horse trader would feed and stable a lame horse, especially no trader as cruel as Hart Latham. A limp was the same as a death sentence.

If she could tend to the injury, Erika was confident that Arany would be all right. Some of the plants here in California were almost exactly like the herbs Naganya used for treating horses back home. She'd seen plenty of waybread, one of the surest remedies for lameness in horses. But would she even be allowed to treat Arany? Would

Hart Latham even listen to her?

Not much chance of that, Erika thought ruefully. To Hart Latham she and her family were nothing but "bohunks," foreigners from remote lands in faraway Europe. He was happy to take their rent money, but whenever he spoke to them he tried to make them feel small and unwelcome.

Erika stood beside the filly, resting a hand lightly on her withers. She felt Arany's hide quiver beneath her touch. What should she do? She couldn't leave her without trying to help. Could she run home, prepare a salve, and bring it back here? But the wrappings would have to be changed regularly. She would never be able to sneak back day after day. Maybe she could—

"What do you think you're doing?"

Erika whirled, and Arany was so startled that she flung up her head and bolted away. A squat, red-faced man in mud-spattered overalls glared from the other side of the fence. "I was just—" Erika stammered. "I—"

"You got no business with them horses," the man growled. "Get out of there!"

On trembling legs, Erika stumbled from the paddock, barely remembering to shut the gate behind her. The man watched her through narrowed eyes. "You're the renter's girl, ain't you?" he said.

Erika straightened her shoulders. "My father is Laszlo Nagy," she said. "We rent land from Mr. Latham."

"You better see the boss," he grunted, motioning for her to follow him. Erika had no choice but to obey. He led her around the back of the massive stone house and told her to wait at the kitchen door. He disappeared inside, and Erika waited alone. The wall of the house blocked the afternoon sun, and the bushes in the door-yard looked feeble and thin. A chill seeped through Erika's light muslin bodice. She paced back and forth, crossing her arms to try to keep warm. *Why would Hart Latham want to see me?* she wondered. Maybe he had found Virag again. Perhaps this time he had carried out his threat!

At last a shadow fell across the doorway, and Hart Latham stepped outside. He was not a tall man, but he made Erika think of a bear, fierce and powerful on its sturdy hind legs. Latham's shirt and trousers were rumpled, and he frowned at her above a tangled dark beard.

"It's about time!" he said, glaring. "I thought I'd have to send Maddox to collect!"

"Collect?" Erika repeated blankly.

"Hand it over!" Latham said. "You better have brought the full amount!"

Erika edged away from him, hiding her empty hands behind her back. "I didn't bring anything," she said. "What amount?"

"No excuses this time!" Latham exploded. "Your father's two months behind on the rent! Where is it?"

Erika's stomach gave a sickening lurch. Why hadn't she guessed that the rent was overdue? Instead of working the land, Papa spent all his time at the gold diggings. She knew they owed money at the store in town. When she worried about it to Papa, he assured her he'd pay off their debt as soon as he made a strike. Joe Muldoon at the store understood miners, Papa said. He was willing to give them credit, knowing he'd be paid soon enough.

It was one thing to owe money to smiling, paunchy Joe Muldoon. It was quite another matter to fall behind on rent to Hart Latham.

Erika drew a deep breath. "Papa didn't tell me about any rent, Mr. Latham. But, listen, one of your horses has a bad leg. The little gold-coloured one. I think I can help—"

"It's my horse," Latham interrupted. "What becomes of her is no business of yours."

"But she'll be lame!" Erika tried once more. "The right plants will help her get better."

Latham gave a short laugh. "You have a lot more to worry about than a horse. Go home and tell your father to bring me the rent by tomorrow morning. If he doesn't pay, you and your family can get off my land!"

The earth seemed to tilt beneath Erika's feet. She thought she was going to faint. "No!" she cried. "We'll pay! Give us a chance!"

Suddenly a voice called from inside, a woman's voice, filled with concern. "Hart! What's going on?"

Latham's tone shifted. It was almost gentle as he replied, "Don't worry, Mags. Everything's all right."

Erika knew in an instant that the slender, fair-haired young woman who slipped out the door had to be Mrs. Latham. Papa had mentioned that Latham had a wife, but she was scarcely ever seen. Erika thought she was very pretty, with dimpled cheeks and soft blue eyes. No wonder Latham kept her out of sight, with so many rough-talking, hard-drinking miners around and so few women at the diggings to keep them company.

"I thought I heard a girl's voice," Mrs. Latham said shyly.

"It's only Nagy's girl," Latham said dismissively. "She has to go now."

"Couldn't she stay and visit a while?" Mrs. Latham asked, a hopeful smile lifting the corners of her mouth.

"Not now. She has a message to deliver for me," Latham said brusquely, with a hard look at Erika. His wife turned reluctantly and slipped into the house again.

Latham looked back at Erika. "Don't just stand there!" he snapped. "Go tell your father what I said!"

Tears stung Erika's eyes. How could she deliver such bad news to Papa? What would he do? If he didn't have the rent money, where would they go?

She ran across the yard, eager to put distance between herself and Hart Latham. "Tomorrow morning!" he hurled after her, and his words struck her like sharp-edged stones.